WWW.BEWAREORMONSTERS.COM

PRAISE FOR J. KENT HOLLOWAY

"Not since Preston & Child's Agent Pendergast has there been a more mysterious, charming and fun to read sleuth as Ezekiel Crane. His mixture of southern charm, dark history and scientific know-how is intoxicating."

—Jeremy Robinson,
international bestselling author of
Project Nemesis

"Holloway skillfully weaves a back-woods tapestry of Sherlock Holmes with TV's *Supernatural* and *Justified* into a thrilling Appalachian story of magic and mayhem. The Dirge amps up the action, menace, and mojo, for a spookfest of epic proportions, with a layered mystery and surprises at every turn. Join Ezekiel Crane, and bring your ten-demon bag for another Dark Hollows adventure. This series somehow got even better."

—Kane Gilmour,
international bestselling author of
The Crypt of Dracula

"*Siren's Song* hits all the right notes. A page-turning plot, heart-stopping battles above and below the waves, cutting-edge technology and weaponry — and of course, more double-crossing villains than you can shake a spear-gun at. Holloway's a skilled conductor, and *Siren's Song* a thrilling symphony."

—David Sakmyster,
international bestselling author of
The Pharos Objective

"Killer mermaids, government conspiracies, and women as beautiful as they are evil. Sirens' Song will lure you to the last page!"

—Rick Chesler,
international bestselling author of
Wired Kingdom

CENTURION

A JACK SIGLER CONTINUUM NOVELLA

JEREMY ROBINSON

WITH J. KENT HOLLOWAY

BREAKNECK MEDIA

Visit Jeremy Robinson on the World Wide Web at:
www.bewareofmonsters.com

Visit J. Kent Holloway on the World Wide Web at:
www.kenthollowayonline.com

ALSO BY JEREMY ROBINSON

ALSO BY J. KENT HOLLOWAY

The Jack Sigler Continuum Series
Guardian
Patriot
Centurion

The ENIGMA Directive Series
Primal Thirst
Sirens' Song
Devil's Child
Savage Frost

The Ezekiel Crane Mystery Series
The Cursed
The Deathsong
The Ghostfeast (coming soon)

The Ajax Clean Thrillers
Clean Exit

Standalone Novels
The Djinn

Short Stories
"Freakshow" (An ENIGMA Directive Short Story)
"Masquerade at One Thousand Feet"
"Haunted Melody" (A Meikle Bay Horror Short Story)

CENTURION

A JACK SIGLER CONTINUUM NOVELLA

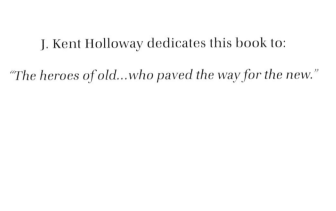

J. Kent Holloway dedicates this book to:

"The heroes of old...who paved the way for the new."

JACK SIGLER: A MAN OUT OF TIME

Jack Sigler was a modern soldier. First for the Army, then for the anti-terror Delta unit known as 'Chess Team' and finally for Endgame, a black budget organization specializing in fending off strange and otherworldly global threats. After several brutal, yet successful, missions, the man known by the callsign: King, found himself torn away from his family and thrust back in time, abandoned in the year 780 BC. But that's not where his life would end. He was gifted with regenerative powers, making him nearly immortal. He heals quickly. Doesn't age. And he was nearly 2800 years away from his daughter and fiancée.

Now, the only way he can return to his own time and his family is to live, fight and sometimes wage war through the oncoming centuries, carrying on his original mission: to protect the weak, right wrongs and send the world's monsters back to whatever hell spawned them.

Centurion, the third tale in the *Jack Sigler Continuum* series, takes place after King has lived in the past for nearly nine hundred years…

1

Celwyn Village of the Silures Tribe
Britannia
AD 102

The madman screamed up at the rain-swept sky, stumbling along the muddy road through the village. His clothes, little more than tattered rags, flapped in the crisp October wind as he convulsed his way into the center of town. His arms flailed, as if batting away a swarm of hungry flies eating his tortured flesh. From the hideous, infected gouges in his face, arms and legs, many of the villagers—quiet farmers and hunters—wondered if he'd lost his mind or if the Devil had claimed him.

Glywn Nashguic, the town's blacksmith, approached the distraught man. "Easy friend." He held up his hands, showing he meant no harm. "We are here to help you."

Three more men, the bravest hunters in the village, eased up to Nashguic's back, their bows and swords ready for a possible fight. The crazed man's eyes narrowed at them, and he let out a pitiful growl.

Nashguic turned to the men behind them, cautioning them with a glance, then turned back to the stranger.

"They do not mean you any harm," he said. Then he saw the bloody, festering wounds covering the man's face. He strained against the urge to vomit. The gouges were more serious than he'd first thought, digging deep into the muscle tissue of the man's cheeks and neck. Each hole squirmed with dozens of tiny maggots, consuming his living flesh with ravenous appetites. The man's lips were dry and cracking, as if he'd not had anything to drink for days. They were split where he'd been chewing on them. "We have a healer here. She can help you."

The man growled again, and took a single step toward him. "N-no one can...help me."

The blacksmith, surprised the madman was capable of speaking, glanced around, catching the other villagers' eyes, peeking out from deep inside the safety of their round mud huts. They stared at the stranger with a toxic mixture of pity, fear and revulsion. The children tugged at their mothers' waists, urging them to hide.

"Sister Clarese can." Nashguic looked back at one of the men standing guard behind him and nodded. Immediately, the man took off in search of the healer. "She is special. Powerful. Maybe the most powerful person in all Britannia. If anyone knows how to cure your ailments, it will be her."

The man swatted away at unseen things, and then glared at Nashguic. Or at least, he appeared to glare. The more the blacksmith looked into the man's eyes, the more he became convinced that it wasn't anger or fury that burned within, but pain.

Angst.

Maybe even shame.

"Y-you need to get your...your people..." The man struggled for the words, like hands held his tongue, trying to keep him from speaking. With a sudden roar, he shook his head as if throwing off restraints and continued. "...get them away from here. Before it is too late."

The bow hunter, Aldryd, stepped to Nashguic's side and nocked his bow. "Is that a threat, stranger?"

Six more men stood around the blacksmith, weapons gripped in their hands.

"No, wait!" Nashguic cried out, but it was too late.

The madman leapt toward them with a roar. Though he was lean—almost bone thin from starvation—he was surprisingly fast. And unnaturally strong. He went for Aldryd the Bowman first. Grabbing Aldryd by his tunic, the stranger lifted him into the air with one hand and hurled him toward two other villagers. He then wheeled around, and disarmed Llyr by grabbing the larger man's forearm and twisting it with a sickening crack. Llyr's short sword fell to the mud.

"Stop! Please!" the blacksmith shouted. "There is no need for this!"

The stranger paused and turned toward Nashguic, then glanced down at the four men writhing on the ground, and at the rest running scared toward their homes. He clenched his eyes shut and sighed.

"Please," the madman said. "Get them to safety. Evil comes this night. And there is nothing I can do to stop it."

With that, and without waiting for the healer to arrive, he bolted away toward the town's gates.

"You are feeble!" a hoarse voice inside the madman's head whispered as he ran through the gate. *"Weak!"*

"You cannot hold onto us much longer," another voice growled. *"Not much longer now. No."*

The man clamped both hands over his ears, struggling to dampen the bantering voices. Thick rain beat against him as he slogged along the trail, moving as fast as his mud-caked bare feet would carry him. He needed to get away from the village and find a secluded hiding place before it was too late. The voices were right. It wouldn't be long now before the *Release*, as he called it, would come. He could hold no more. He now contained more of the dark spirits than he had at any time before in his long past. His soul was tearing from the strain. "I will hold you...for as long...as I can."

"It will not be enough," a voice said.

"Never ever enough," another said.

"No, no, no. Not ever. Never. Ever enough," the first repeated.

"Your guilt," a third, much deeper, more bestial voice said. *"Your guilt is ambrosia to us, mortal. We feed upon it. It strengthens us. Even now..."*

"Even now...we ready ourselves for your world." This last sentence seemed to come from all of the voices ricocheting throughout his head. *"For our glorious hunt!"*

They were right, and the man knew it. The more his guilt consumed him, the stronger they grew, and the quicker he would have to release them to ease the agonizing burden. More lives would be lost because of his weakness. And his guilt would only increase.

He had to end this. Had to find a way to put this horrible curse to rest once and for all.

He scurried down the lane, just outside the village, and he began making his way toward the up-stretched pine spires of the forest to the east. *There will be no graves there,* he thought, seeking to deprive the spirits of the resources they needed.

"A wasted effort, Centurion. Your kind is like vermin to this world. You breed like rabbits and feed like cockroaches."

"You are everywhere. Filling holes in the ground."

"We love the holes."

"So many nice, little holes…"

"Filled with bones…"

"You cannot be free of us without the consequences that torment you so."

"Oh, God, help me," the man said, just before his toes caught against a tree root jutting up from the ground, propelling him into the mud.

The voices in his head cackled. *"How many times must we tell you, Child of Cain?"*

"After what you did…"

"…there will be no help from Him."

"We promise you that. You are ours…"

"…to play with as we see fit!"

The man pushed himself up from the mud, and stumbled forward again—determined to make it to the forest before the unthinkable could happen.

Again.

"Leave me alone!"

The voices' laughter grew louder.

How many times in the last seventy years had he uttered those very words? And each time, he received the same response. Laughter. Mockery. The demons weren't lying about one thing…he was their plaything. To do whatever was necessary to torment him for the evil thing he'd done those many years before. He couldn't argue with the punishment, however. He deserved it. He had, after all, in his great hubris, performed one of the most heinous of acts. And there was no doubt he deserved to suffer for all eternity.

But why do the innocents suffer? Why must they endure my torment along with me?

"Guilt!" one of the voices cried.

"So succulent!"

"So tasty!"

"The more you wonder," the deepest voice said, *"the more delectable the meal."*

"And soon, we will be feeding on flesh once more…"

"Men are even more savory than guilt!"

With a scream, the man who was considered mad by all who met him—the man who'd once been a great soldier for the Roman military war machine, and who had spent the last seventy years in seclusion—ran as fast as he could. Though his guilt fueled the wills of those that tormented him, it also strengthened his resolve.

He would not release them in a populated area ever again. Would not provide them with the means to enter the mortal realm they so desperately craved. It was precisely why he'd traveled so far into this 'No Man's Land'…this Britannia. The population was minuscule compared to the other regions of the Empire. Fewer people to fall prey to the evil that resided within him.

With renewed vigor, he sprinted toward the woods. To safety. To seclusion. All that was needed now was to crest a small hill up ahead and he would be clear.

He would be free.

The man ran. Legs and arms pumping wildly. Droplets of rain pelted against his forehead, but he paid the chill they brought no heed. Thunder boomed overhead, but he was unaware of it. He was driven by a single purpose. A single need to protect the village behind him.

He ignored the voices' taunts. Ignored their accusations. And he moved ever closer to that hill. The small hump in the earth just at the foot of the tree line. The small round patch of earth that…

He skidded to a halt the moment he realized his mistake. He hadn't been running toward freedom. His mind—clouded as it was by the spirit creatures imprisoned within him—had directed him to the one place he knew he must *not* go. The one place that was the most dangerous for him to tread.

The hill was, after all, no ordinary hill.

It was a mound.

A burial mound.

A cairn.

The voices' hissing laughter filled his head. They were overjoyed, and the more glee they felt, the stronger his sense of failure became. Guilt, once again, over failing to avoid the Release, as he'd so desperately hoped. Guilt over knowing what would happen to the poor villagers.

"Fine," he said, crumpling to his knees and offering a resigned sigh. "Let it begin."

2

Though he had experienced the Release many times before, it was no less excruciating. The moment the convulsions came, the madman fell to his back and thrashed about on the ground, as hundreds of new sores erupted over his entire body. In tortured agony, the man shredded the remainder of his tunic and breeches away, then he screamed into the howling wind of the storm.

Rain beat down on him from above, pummeling his body, as a blazing ribbon of lightning slashed at the heavens. His desperate screams drowned out the rumbling thunder, as hundreds of tiny, imperceptible mouths tore chunks of muscle and skin from his body. White, writhing bodies began wriggling out from the newly formed ulcers, dropping to the ground—a flesh-eating waterfall. The man shuddered as each new sore burst outward from his insides. Unwelcome tears streaked his face, salt water mixing with the rain drenching his body.

Another streak of lightning arced across the sky, illuminating the ever darkening afternoon landscape. Each flash highlighted the writhing mass of larvae as they dropped from his pain-addled form and squirmed their way toward the funerary cairn.

"No!" the man screamed. "Do not do this! Please!"

But all the voices, except one, had been silenced the moment the worms ate their way out of him. He'd expected as much. This was how it always was. The worms left to bring torment to the world. One worm, as always, remained behind—already pregnant with hundreds of new eggs ready to wreak havoc.

With burning red eyes, he watched the tiny white creatures inching and hopping their way, almost end over end, toward the mound. The sight of the procession ripped away at the last vestiges of his sanity, as easily as the worms had rent his very flesh asunder. Both his mind and body had been shredded to pieces, as if the talons of some great raptor had laid claim to his very soul. He felt hollowed out. Nothing left of the man he was before all this began.

He glanced at the mound. The maggots were still pouring from his gaping sores. Disgusted, he assaulted as many of them as he could with long, jagged fingernails. Though he managed to destroy a few, he did even more damage to his body. He didn't care. Frustrated, and in agonizing pain, he continued scraping at his own flesh. Long red welts blossomed up and down his skin as he raked his nails back and forth along his arms. But the larvae continued to come.

"Just let me die!" he sobbed. "Just let me die. Please."

He was gasping for air now. Exhaustion and muscle fatigue were taking hold.

"*NO.*"

The voice was loud. It seemed audible, and not inside his own mind. A mixture of all the voices he knew—and a few he did not—that had shared his body for such a long time. The remaining parent and the unborn larvae. Already they were strong enough to communicate their vile hatred to him.

He rolled over onto his side, his hands now clutching his gut as a terrible spasm ripped through his abdomen. His tear-filled eyes fell to the muddy soil all around him and the innumerable worms still digging their way inside the burial mound.

He ground his teeth and sat up, focusing on that very familiar and unfamiliar voice.

"But...but why?" he asked aloud, uncertain whether they could hear his thoughts any more.

"*We have told you before.*"

"*So many times before.*"

"*Yes. So many times.*"

"*YOU ARE A SON OF CAIN.*"

"*Yes. And also...*"

"*...we are your mother.*"

"*Would you separate...*"

"*...a mother...*"

"...from her child?"

The man coughed. A spray of spittle mixed with blood exploded from his mouth, as the last of the larvae oozed their way out of a new wound in his navel.

"I am not your..." *Cough. Cough.* "...child! Why are you doing this?"

But they didn't answer him. Instead, they continued to crawl and burrow into the wet soil with a single-minded purpose, leaving him only with despair to keep him company.

Almost all the maggots had now burrowed into the cairn. Only a few remained.

There are thousands of them, he thought.

The pain had finally subsided, and he found himself able to breathe easily again. But no matter how badly he might desire it, they would never allow him to die. As a matter of fact, he knew the mother was already working on mending the wounds. Protecting him from infection. Knitting him back together...as good as new. She would keep him alive and well so that more of their kind could feed off his anguish. *Thousands. I have never seen so many before.* The thought sent a chill down his spine. He could only imagine the monstrosity that would emerge once they had consumed the remains from inside the grave.

In the past, the most he'd ever released were two or three hundred, and the nightmare creatures they had formed had devastated everything in their wake. The thought of what thousands could do was enough to fray the remaining tatters of his sanity.

He took a deep breath, trying to calm himself. He was beginning to feel the strength come back to his arms and legs. Not the supernatural god-like strength he experienced whenever *they* inhabited his body *en masse*, but the normal, everyday human strength. The strength of a healthy thirty-year-old male...which was still rather impressive consider-ing he was currently one hundred and four years old.

A crack of thunder boomed overhead, jolting him back to his current predicament. He glanced at the burial mound. Something rumbled beneath the earth on which he lay.

Do I stay and fight? He craned his head behind him, toward the village he'd just fled. *Should I warn them again? They did not listen to me the first time.* He turned and looked past the mound, at the lush forest beyond. *Or do I just run? Like I always do.*

Like I never stop doing.

The sound of stone and dirt crackled underneath him, just before something long and black slithered out from the moist soil. The object writhed, back and forth, before two more similar objects—*tentacles?*—began wriggling up from the cairn. Then, the burial mound began to bubble over, as something massive churned and tossed at the dirt that encompassed it.

"By the gods," the man muttered, his eyes widening at the sight. In all the years he'd endured his curse, he'd never seen anything like the creature slowly burrowing its way to the surface. Still recovering from the extreme physical exertion that wracked his body, he clambered to his feet, then began edging backward. Though every instinct in his body screamed for him to run into the woods and escape this new demonic beast, his legs refused to comply. Refused to even approach the writhing mound of dirt.

He cursed himself. He'd once been a great warrior. Fearless. Feared by others. Brutal. He'd served Caesar with honor on numerous occasions, and he'd made his ancestors proud with each victory. Then came that horrid day in Jerusalem. He'd been little more than a cowering mess ever since.

Now he was too afraid to run past the thing forming in front of him, yet too ashamed to run back to the village to warn them once more.

It was too late, after all.

He knew it.

There was nothing to be done about this creature— or maybe *creatures*. He couldn't quite tell yet.

"Go, child of mine," the voice echoed through his thoughts, as if a clap of thunder had been compressed into a deep cavern. *"Warn them. It makes it all the more entertaining when they run. Or better, when they fight."*

There was a chorus of child-like snickers that caught on the wind, then the voice continued. *"The Sluagh come. The Hunt is about to begin."*

When the creatures spoke their name, it was inevitably stretched out, as *slooo-aaah*. But the other word caught his attention.

"Hunt? What do you mean...hunt?" This was only the second time—and in a single conversation—that he'd heard them use the term. Of course, it was only recently that they had become so verbose. For most of the decades he'd been imprisoned by them, they had remained perfectly silent, and he wondered what had changed to cause their sudden desire to converse with him.

The choir of laughter repeated, this time more boisterous than before. *"Well, Centurion. What game do you think we have been playing over the years?"*

Another voice, this one higher pitched, almost feminine and far less sane, seemed to speak from somewhere off to his left. *"Not just to torment you. No. No. No. Though that has been quite enthralling. We seek...we desire...we crave...to spread the torment all around. We hunt. We feast. We build upon that which we harvest."*

"The Hunt continues," the deeper voice said. *"And you have been our faithful steed for nearly a century now."*

Three more tentacles slithered up from the ground as the bulge at the mound's crest continued to expand. Whatever was beneath was about to reveal itself.

The feminine voice neighed, imitating a horse. *"Faithful steed. Horsey. Horsey. We love our Horsey Horse. We will never let him go."*

"Run along, steed. Go warn yon village, so the Hunt may begin anew!"

"Shoo. Anew. Shoo. Anew!" the female voice sang. *"It is time for blood and fear and pain. Shoo, shoo, shoo!"*

Now truly terrified, the man turned from the churning mound and ran toward the small village. He had no hope of saving lives. And no illusions as to the town's chances. But he ran nonetheless. Not for any altruistic reasons, but rather because he had nowhere else to run. He was the Sluagh's steed, after all. They would find him no matter where he was stabled. It was time to accept his own doom.

3

**Celwyn Village of the Silures Tribe
Britannia
Three Days Later**

The three weary travelers stopped at the burning town's gate; its doors had been torn from the hinges and tossed to the ground. They peered through the opening, taking in the smoldering ruins. Acrid black smoke wafted past them in billowing gusts.

"Looks like we are in the right place," said the short rotund man dressed in thick red bishop's robes. He repositioned himself on the saddle of his horse, attempting to ease the immense pressure on his backside. "It looks as though the Sluagh only recently swept through here."

"Always one step ahead of us," said the lean, hard-faced man in the middle. He was dressed in the gleaming bronze battle armor of a Roman Centurion, with his long crimson cloak whisking solemnly behind him. He removed his plumed helmet and scanned the landscape.

As usual, the warrior was as taciturn as a desert stone, and the bishop couldn't help but ponder just how scarred the poor man's soul must be. He had endured much during his long life.

"Are we going to sit here all day, or are we going to investigate?" the third traveler said. He was younger, by far, than the other two riders. But neither of his companions saw his youth as a detriment. Despite having lived less than twenty short years, the lean, wiry tracker had been a tremendous asset during their search for the demonic scourge cutting a swath of destruction from Jerusalem to the British Isles. He did, however, tend to be overly enthusiastic from time to time. "I do not know about you two, but I have been straddling this ungodly beast for far too long. I need to stretch my legs. Catch a whiff of the monsters' scents, if I can."

He lifted his right leg, preparing to dismount from his horse when he was stopped by a firm word from the centurion.

"Hold, Skilurus," the centurion said, holding up his right fist and cocking his head to the right, as if straining to hear something just out of audible range. "Something isn't right." He turned to the bishop. "Polycarp, do you sense it?"

The famed Bishop of Smyrna knew precisely what he was asking. Something supernatural was still lurking about the desiccated and charred human remains. He could sense it. It was both his gift and curse since becoming a believer in the man his mentor, Johannes, taught him about, the lord Christus. He had the unnatural ability to sense the presence of supernatural forces. To his knowledge, he was only one of a handful of believers with the ability, and it had proven useful on more than one occasion since their search began. But the accursed man known only as Longinus—a former centurion who had been present at the Crucifixion of the Lord—was an elusive target.

"Aye, Ursus. Though I cannot quite pinpoint what it is, something does indeed remain here. We best be on our guard, and search the village for any survivors. If there are any, we must tend to their injuries and see if they can tell us what has happened here." His nose crinkled at the sight and smell assaulting his senses. "In all our travels, I have never seen the demons cause this kind of destruction. This is different. More sinister."

The centurion nodded his head, pulled a well-honed antique Grecian sword from the scabbard on his back and dismounted. He then silently nodded to Skilurus, who followed suit. "Stay on your horse, Padre," he said. Though Polycarp's official title was 'Episkopos', or Bishop, the warrior had refused to call him that since the day they'd met. He'd opted for the less formal 'priest' or the foreign word 'padre'. Either, in fact, was perfectly fine with the Smyrnan bishop, who cared little for titles. "We'll do some reconnaissance, check for threats and come back for you."

"I think not!" Polycarp scrambled from his steed and wheeled around, directing a defiant glare at the centurion. He crossed his arms over his chest, but his short arms could hardly stretch over his ample belly. "You may have need of me, warrior, though even after all this time you might still doubt my worth. But I will not cower to this hellacious scourge. Do we understand each other?"

The man now known as Centurion Ursus Rex glared at the bishop, the muscles of his jaw flexing back and forth as he considered the ultimatum. After several uncomfortable moments, the Roman soldier gave a curt nod, stalked past the city gate, and came to an abrupt halt. Moments later, the two others sidled up next to him and awaited his orders.

Ursus's eyes darted left and right. The muscles of his entire body seemed rigid and ready to spring should the need arise.

"What do you sense, *Padre*?"

There was that name again. To Polycarp, it sounded very similar to the Latin *Pater*—father—but for the life of him, the bishop could not understand the correlation. In the end, he'd decided long ago to just accept the warrior's strange language quirks and move on.

"As I said, there *is* a presence here," he said. "Though it is odd. Like an echo that has not quite played itself out. There is evil here, that much I know. But..."

"Skilurus?" Ursus cut the priest off. "Do your thing."

The young man's eyes widened before suddenly snapping to attention. "Really? I mean...you are going to let me..."

Ursus stretched out a hand, and swept it around to encompass the entire village. Bodies—torn asunder and being shredded by carrion birds, along with mongrels and maggots alike, littered the muddy streets. The smoldering embers of a town-wide fire still glimmered here and there, flaring up with each new gust of wind. Flies buzzed back and forth, creating a constant hum, smothering all other sounds.

"We don't have time to do this the hard way, kid. We could spend days searching the ruins for survivors...or any of the creatures that might still be lurking around." The centurion shrugged. "And as much as I hate it when you...when you do your *special* thing, it does have its advantages." He spun around, jabbing a sturdy index finger against the boy's chest. "Just don't get all Teen Wolf on me, and we'll be okay. Got it?"

Skilurus, oblivious to the reference, nodded enthusiastically.

"I'm serious, kid. I see one hair on your head grow an iota longer..." He hefted his ancient sword. "...you'll be due for a haircut."

"How can I? You burned my cloak in Glynnard," the boy said, and he was met with an immediate glare. Skilurus held up his hands. "I can no longer fully change. You know better than anyone. But I promise I will keep it under control. I promise."

The bishop smiled at the exchange. He'd taken an almost instant liking to Skilurus since he and Ursus had met the boy nearly nine months before. They'd heard rumors of a young man who'd been inflicted by a terrible curse in the region of Scythia. Believing the tales might be related to Longinus, the two had set out to investigate, only to discover a nearly feral boy, mad from some malady that made him believe himself to be a wolf. Upon first seeing Skilurus, Polycarp had almost been convinced himself. Though it had been dark, the streets thick with shadows, upon their first encounter, the bishop would have sworn the young man's snout had been elongated and his body covered with hair. But Ursus had tracked him down and captured the young man with very little trouble. By the time they brought the boy into the light, the near-starving youth looked perfectly normal, and the bishop had felt a kinship to him.

The reverse was true for Ursus Rex, who had taken an immediate dislike to Skilurus. Or rather, he had originally placed little to no trust in him. He'd only agreed to allow him to join them on their journey to keep a sharp eye on him, lest he revert to his old ways. One night, in the wee hours after they'd both had a little too much wine, the Roman warrior had confided in the bishop that he'd met others like Skilurus.

Many, many years previously. People from a land known as Scythia—the *Neuri*, he called them—who supposedly could transform into wolves once every year and commit heinous acts against nearby villages.

Ursus believed young Skilurus to be a descendent of these people. Even more unsettling, Skilurus seemed to share in the belief. Polycarp, of course, thought the very idea was preposterous. He sensed no evil in the boy, and to be able to transform into a wolf would surely require the forces of Hell itself. More than likely, Skilurus had simply been mad with hunger when they'd first encountered him, which had played into the warrior's old fashioned superstitions. Either way, the bishop was glad he'd agreed to allow Skilurus to join them in their quest. It had simply been serendipity that he'd proven to be an excellent tracker who had assisted them on more than one occasion during their travels.

Perhaps Ursus was finally beginning to see that as well. Despite Polycarp's encouragement, the centurion had never placed much trust in the boy. Had never offered him a task truly worthy of his skills. And now, in this accursed place, it seemed Skilurus would finally get his chance to do something real.

"You ready?" Ursus's question to Skilurus brought the bishop back to the present.

The lad grinned from ear to ear, planted his feet wide apart and gave a self-assured nod.

"Go."

At the centurion's command, the boy bolted from his spot—almost running through the muddy road on all fours—and dashed through the village in a blur. Ursus turned to the bishop with a roll of his eyes. "We better follow before the kid gets himself in some serious trouble."

4

The village's interior had not been spared the destructive siege that had befallen the outskirts. No matter where the companions looked, carnage lurked. Bodies lay strewn about. Their limbs twisted in physically impossible angles. Their entrails, ripped loose through gaping wounds in their abdomens, hung along clothes lines, where ravens gorged themselves on the putrefying flesh.

"Shoo! Shoo!" Polycarp shouted, waving his arms in the air. "Nasty beasts." He glanced over at his companion. "Full of evil in their own right, I would wager."

The centurion ignored the comment. He had once been known as Jack Sigler, callsign: King, of an elite Delta unit called Chess Team, and had been flung back in time, condemned to live out the years as an immortal until he returned to his own time. Instead of responding to the bishop, he kept his gaze fixed on young Skilurus, as the young man ran through the village. The boy sniffed the air every so often before returning to the hunt. King had seen many strange things during his now long life, but the young man and his people were high on the list. They weren't exactly the modern—in his time, anyway—definition of werewolves, but they were as close to any he'd seen. They didn't physically transform, but would rather slip into a wolfskin cloak and alter their perception to the point where, mentally, they would become wolf-like. They'd even developed incredible heightened senses, allowing them to scent out their prey. When the 'madness' struck, they were endowed with incredible strength and endurance. The downside, of course, was the madness itself. Once a year, for unknown reasons, it would strike each of the boy's kind—making them completely unmanageable and infinitely more dangerous. Once in a while, even when it wasn't during the winter equinox, the madness would strike if the individual tapped into the 'wolf' for too long. It was this danger that made King so wary of letting Skilurus run wild.

He knew Polycarp didn't understand. But then, he'd never fought the boy's ancestors in ancient Scythia either. King, on the other hand, had. He knew just how dangerous these lycanthropes could be. Though down deep, he liked and admired the kid, King had little qualms about ending his life should the beast within grow out of control. He'd mourn the loss. He'd carry the guilt on his conscience for centuries. But should the need arise, he wouldn't hesitate. Skilurus knew and understood that, which only endeared him to King even more, if he allowed himself to admit it.

"How many bodies have you counted so far?" King asked, walking over and crouching next to the body of a young girl—no more than fifteen years old. He brushed a strand of mud-encrusted hair from her face. Though they looked nothing alike, King couldn't help but conjure images of his adopted daughter, Fiona, to mind. He clenched his teeth at the vision, and turned toward the bishop.

"So far...not counting random body parts impossible to match to any one individual, I have counted thirty-six."

King closed his eyes, allowed himself a brief sigh, then stood up and looked at the bishop. "I'm tired of this, Padre. I'm tired of these...these whatever they are..."

"Demons."

"They're not demons. They're something else. They've got to be."

Polycarp shrugged. "I realize you are not prone to believing in anything inexplicable to the sciences, Ursus. But trust me. There are things out there that can be understood only by faith. The people of this land would agree with you. To them, these creatures are not demons. To them, they are the Sluagh—the congregated dead of evil men. Sinners so vile that Hell itself is said to have spat them out. Men so vicious even the earth repels them, not allowing their spirits to wander unaided over the ground. They require vessels to move about, and in their true form, they fly on wings of smoke and brimstone. In Germania, they are more akin to something called the Wild Hunt—a group of spirits that fly upon the winds of the night, hunting down poor unfortunate souls. Other tribes and nations may know them by different names. I, however, prefer the much simpler term, *demon*."

"Well, the point is, if we don't find and put an end to Longinus soon, I'm going to need a..."

"Master Ursus! Master Polycarp!" Skilurus's voice echoed through the forest of burned timbers that had once framed the village's round homes. "Come quick! I have found something!"

King gave the bishop a questioning gaze, then darted toward the young man's voice. As he ran, he could hear the overweight priest heave for breath, trying to keep up. Despite the man's age, vocation and level of fitness, Polycarp had surprised King on many occasions with his bravery and determination. And his uncanny knack for sensing all things evil had come in handy more times than he could count. He only wished the theologian wasn't so ready to accept the realm of the supernatural and evil spirits as the cause of so many of the creatures they'd encountered over the years. It would make things much simpler between them.

It wasn't that King didn't believe. He did. He had gone to Sunday School as a kid. Had grown up with a deep respect for the 'Man Upstairs'. But like most twenty-first century adults, he had discovered a great many more things to concern himself with once he'd matured. Granted, his time in the past had only helped to cement his views of God. He'd just seen too many things not to believe. But he'd also seen too many monsters. Too much evil to contend with to ever really have the time to reflect on God's place in his life. If he hadn't been such a pragmatist, he would have laughed at the irony of an immortality with too little time.

King set these thoughts aside as he rounded a corner to see Skilurus crouching beside a man covered in blood and grime. The man, dressed in little more than torn rags, clutched at his gut. He rocked back and forth as the kid cradled him in his lap.

"He is alive," Skilurus said. "He does not look injured either. But I think he is in pain."

King stepped cautiously toward the man, his sword leveled and ready to swing, should the man suddenly attack. King had heard too many tales of these Sluagh creatures feigning injuries or illness to lure the unwary within their reach. He wouldn't make that mistake.

But if Polycarp shared his concerns, he didn't show it. Instead, the bishop brushed past King and knelt beside the man. Reaching into his pouch, he retrieved a clean cloth, then dowsed it with water from his water bladder. He began cleaning the man's face while whispering soothing words into his ears.

"You are going to be all right," he whispered. "We are here now. The Lord comes before us. He has looked after you until we were able to arrive."

The man began to wail mournfully at the bishop's words.

"Shhhh. Quiet, now." Polycarp brushed a lock of the man's greasy unkempt hair from his face and gasped. He didn't have to say anything for King to know what had surprised him. The man's face was pitted by hundreds of red, pus-filled holes. Here and there, bobbing in and out, King could just make out the sickening white heads of maggots protruding from the sores. The bishop looked over at Skilurus. "He may not be injured from battle, young one, but he is far from healthy. Quick, help me pick him up. We need to find him a place to rest, so I can tend to his illness."

"Padre." King's one word conveyed a dozen thoughts, questions and warnings.

Polycarp gave a nod. "I too sense the evil within this man. He is exactly who you suspect. And no, we will not leave him for the ravens and mongrels to feast upon. We will save this man if we are able." The bishop turned to King and fixed an unwavering glare at him. "Now, do *we* understand each other?"

"I thought our mission was to end this plague sweeping the world," King said, before pointing to the sick man still cradled in Skilurus's lap. "He's the source. He's the one responsible for all of this."

"No, he is not, and you know it, full well." The bishop staggered to his feet, dusting his robes off at the knees.

Then he looked up to King. "He is as much a victim as anyone. More so."

"He's dangerous."

"And so are you, warrior. The most dangerous man alive, I would wager. Do you see me calling for your head because of it?"

"You forget. I don't work for you, Padre. I'm under orders from the Emperor himself...to slay the scourge at its source."

"Which emperor?" The fat man waddled up to King, carefully placing a finger against the shining metal of his armor. "Seems to me, you have served many in the past, no? You have served several generations of Caesars. That is suspicious enough in its own right. Enough for me to suspect you of cavorting with the powers of darkness, too.

"Besides, I have heard the stories. You have defied emperors plenty of times in the past...if the cause was just. I say, you allow me to tend to this man until he is well enough to explain his actions and the curse that follows him. Then, we can decide what to do with him."

King struggled with how to respond. He had no idea the Bishop of Smyrna had known his secret. He'd certainly never alluded to it before today. But despite that, he knew Polycarp was correct. He *had* defied several Caesars in the past. As a matter of fact, he'd tried to stand up to injustice wherever it occurred. Yes, he had failed to do the right thing occasionally. Had lived so long he'd frequently forgotten who he was, where he'd come from and the values that had been instilled in Jack Sigler from an early age. But those values always seemed to come back when it really mattered most. And that was precisely the reason he appreciated his latest companion so much. It was the thing that made Polycarp even more valuable than his courage or supernatural sensitivity. It was his ability to keep King focused on what was right that had proven so indispensable in recent days.

After a moment, King offered a quick nod. "We'll find refuge. A place where he can recuperate. We'll decide what to do with him when he's better."

The bishop smiled, clapping King on the shoulder before turning to help Skilurus lift the mysterious man onto King's shoulder's, to remove him from the village he had somehow destroyed.

5

As King hefted the sick man onto his shoulders and began striding toward the town's gates, an ear-splitting shriek erupted beyond the fortified walls. The trio stopped at the sound, looking for the haunting cry's source.

"It is getting dark," Skilurus said, his dagger clutched in his right hand.

"I can see that," King replied, beginning to walk as fast as he could to their horses. The kid was right. The sun had slipped down past the twenty-foot city walls, casting them into a long shadow. The sky above was a painted canvas of oranges and purples that deepened in shades as it spread high above the few clouds overhead. "We need to move."

Another screech. This one was much closer. Only yards away, if King was any judge of distance.

"Padre?"

"Yes. They are here, Ursus. Though perhaps only a handful remain."

King glanced around, weighing his options. The gate was much too far away. They wouldn't be able to reach the horses before the Sluagh arrived. And in the dimming light, seeing them—in his limited experience fighting the monsters—would be extremely difficult. They needed to find shelter, and fast. Neither the bishop nor the boy were ready to take on multiple Sluagh. And with his arms full, carrying the cursed ex-centurion, he wouldn't do much better. Problem was, as he looked around, he could find none of the village's buildings intact enough to offer any protection. Most of the huts were little more than timbers jutting up from the earth. No roofs. No walls. Just charred shards of wood, macabre caricatures of skeletal remains that were still smoking from the recent fire that set the town ablaze.

King looked at Skilurus and gave a reluctant sigh. "I've got no choice here, Skil. I need your help again."

The boy stepped up with a spring in his step. Though his eyes betrayed just how scared he was, he remained eager to prove himself to King.

Three more shrieks erupted from just as many directions. A sick putrid stench drifted toward them, carried by the unseasonably warm breeze. The creatures were almost on top of them.

"Quickly. Take him." King slipped Longinus from his shoulders—not an entirely difficult task considering how emaciated the poor man was—and handed him to Skilurus. The boy ducked down and scooped the man up onto his own, leaner shoulders. "Find a safe place to hide. Your sense of smell should help you to maneuver around them. Polycarp's gift should be of help as well. Stay low and out of sight, and I'll..."

"You are not planning on fighting them by yourself, are you?" the bishop asked. "I said there were not many of them, but a few is more than enough to..."

"I won't argue with you about this." King shoved the large man toward Skilurus. "They'll need your help more than I will. Now go!"

The bishop looked at King, then at Skilurus and Longinus before nodding. Then, the two of them ran southwest, between the ruins of two huts, before the bishop and the boy disappeared from view. If he had the faith of his theologian friend, he might have offered up a prayer for their safety. Instead, King slung his shield around from where it had been strapped over his cloak, spread his feet apart and prepared for the impending attack.

He didn't have to wait long.

Polycarp heaved for breath as he trailed the leaner, more fit Skilurus through the street. His feet sank into several inches of mud with each step, making the going more difficult. Darkness had fallen quickly, and now he found himself struggling to see the lad only a few feet ahead of him. His hearing, however, was perfectly fine, and he could hear the maddening cries of the Sluagh as they converged on where they'd left Ursus behind.

He prayed that he'd not made a mistake by leaving the centurion to fend for himself. Granted, Ursus was no ordinary man. The bishop wasn't entirely certain he was a man at all. Though he'd kept it to himself during the time they'd known each other, the bishop knew all too well the reputation Ursus Rex—a name that meant the Bear King—had developed over the years. The stories he'd heard of the *Man Who Could Not Die*... It was precisely for that reason he'd sought Ursus out three years before; or rather, it was why his teacher, the Last Apostle, Johannes, had instructed Polycarp to seek him.

Still, surely the stories were merely hyperbole. Exaggerated tales of a great warrior. After all, was it not believed that Johannes was immortal because of one cryptic comment made by the Christus? And yet, the apostle had indeed died. Polycarp had been there at his death bed. He'd seen Johannes take his last breath. If the Lord saw fit to take such a great man as the Revelator of Patmos, surely this godless warrior couldn't truly be invincible.

Could he?

Polycarp had to admit, he'd seen the Roman soldier survive injuries that would have killed lesser men. But come to think of it, he couldn't remember a single time he'd seen any of their enemies come close to striking a mortal blow. Ursus Rex was just too good a fighter for that and...

"Umph!" Distracted by his thoughts, the bishop had failed to see Skilurus stop ahead of him. They'd collided into each other with enough force to nearly bowl the smaller man down. Fortunately, the lad's balance and agility kept him upright long enough for him to spin around, crinkling his brow at the old man, before placing an index finger to lips for silence. It was then that Polycarp noticed the foul smell lingering in the air around them. The stench of decay. His eyes watered at the odor, and he struggled against the rising bile edging up his throat.

"They are here," he whispered.

The boy nodded, then pointed ahead and to the right with his chin. Polycarp looked around. The nearest building was just three feet to their left, but there was no more cover inside than any of the other dozen dwellings they'd passed since leaving the centurion behind. Silently, the boy moved over to the ruins, crouched down and laid the ill man on the ground behind an overturned wooden table. "Keep watch over him," Skilurus whispered. "I will lead them away."

"I cannot let you..."

But before he could finish the sentence, the boy snarled, turned and sprinted away. Before the shadows engulfed him, Polycarp could have sworn Skilurus's facial features had sprouted a bristling patch of hair over his cheeks and chin. Convincing himself it was a trick of the light, the bishop crept into the nearby domicile, sat down next to Longinus and began ministering to his ill charge as best he could. As he continued to clean the strange-looking holes pocking the man's face, he prayed a series of silent prayers for his two endangered friends.

King stood his ground as six human-shaped, hunched-over shadows ambled toward him from the front and the rear. His only means of escape was through the street taken by Skilurus and the Padre, but he had no intention of using it. Despite the fact he and Polycarp had been hunting Longinus and the Sluagh for the last three years, he'd only seen a handful of the creatures in all that time. He'd always arrived too late whenever the scourge appeared. The few he had encountered were as varied as insects scurrying away after a log was lifted from the ground. He'd also heard stories from survivors. Talked to dozens of witnesses. Listened to the descriptions. None of that prepared him for what he saw coming toward him now.

From the survivors he'd interviewed, he knew this particular breed now stalking him should hardly be a danger to him. From what he'd heard, these particular creatures—he'd taken to calling them goblins, based on eyewitness accounts—seemed to be the Sluagh's grunts. Dumb as rocks, but extremely difficult to kill. Fortunately, unlike King, they weren't said to regenerate.

If he could only stifle the gag reflex caused by their stench long enough to deal with them, he'd be fine.

They attacked all at once, darting out into the light of the rising moon. Six dwarf-like creatures, their heads barely coming up to his waist, looked as if they'd been thrown together at a discount body parts store. They were patch-work people—comprised of the limbs, torsos, sinews and flesh of multiple, decaying bodies. Less zombie, more goblin-sized Frankenstein monsters. Their faces were gnarled, bloated caricatures, dark green with marbled, veined flesh. The few remaining eyes among the bunch appeared milky white. Cloudy. The others were merely dried-out husks or hollowed sockets infested with a wriggling mass of larvae.

Besides their diminutive size, which King theorized was due to a lack of human tissue used to fabricate their bodies, they looked very much human. Except for their mouths. To him, their mouths were probably the most alien, demonic things he'd ever seen. And this, coming from a man who'd battled giant scorpion men several centuries earlier, not to mention the Hydra more than a thousand years in the future. There was just something about the shapes of the mouths that unnerved him.

It looked as if the creature's lips had been torn at the corners with sharp claws, forcing their faces into a hideous death's head grin. Only there were no gleaming white teeth to finish the illusion. Instead, hundreds of squirming worms writhed in a circular gum-like nub that jutted slightly from their gaping jaws.

The worms hissed, creating a horrific symphony that nearly drowned out any other sound around him. Protruding no more than a centimeter or so from their cadaverous gums, the squirming mess of maggots bobbed left and right, as if they were gauging King's position through blind eyes.

But the worms weren't content to just sway back and forth and hiss to their black hearts' content. Before he could get a better look at the creatures, the toothlike worms exploded from their mouths, stretching out as elongated, barbed tentacles. The simultaneous strike was so sudden, King barely had time to dodge the first onslaught. When the second barrage of tentacles came, he was more prepared. Sidestepping the nearest creature's attack, he spun around just in time to fend off another blow with his shield. The barbed tips of seven different worm-tentacles embedded themselves into the bronze, nearly loosening his grip on the shield's leather handles. He ducked just before another strike came from behind. Letting his momentum do most of the work, he wheeled around and lopped off the squirming appendage before it could recoil back into the creature's mouth.

The other three goblins lunged toward King when they were close enough. Their powerful jaws clamped down hard on his sword arm, shoulder and right leg. With a shout of pain, he brought his sword down on the head of the beast eating away at the flesh of his leg. The blade bit into the creature's skull, producing a spray of gelatinous black fluid. The thing released its grip to howl, giving King the time he needed to toss his shield aside, grasp the creature by the throat and use it as a bludgeon against its own comrades. With three of his foes down, but not completely out of the fight, he glanced down at his bare legs, just above the straps of his sandaled boots. Three writhing maggots had escaped their hosts and were now busy burrowing themselves into the calves of his leg.

He slapped his palm against his leg, crushing two of them with a sickening smack. The third one, however, slipped through the hole it had burrowed into the muscle and disappeared. Because of his unnatural ability to regenerate, the hole sealed itself up before he could do anything to stop the larvae's progression into his body.

Okay, he thought, as he returned his attention to the attacking Sluagh. *That* can't *be good.*

6

Skilurus vaulted the four-foot tall fence as the creature's giant fist crashed down into the mud, leaving a crater the size of a melon in its wake. The boy tucked his legs up to his chest and rolled forward before coming back up in a full sprint.

When he'd decided to lead the creature away from Longinus and Polycarp, he'd had no idea the trouble he was running toward. He had, after all, never seen the Sluagh before. None of the stories the bishop had told him could have prepared him for the truth. The beast was monstrous— nearly ten feet tall and half as wide, with exaggerated fore- arms as big as tree trunks. Its elongated torso and tiny, dis- proportionately short legs made the thing resemble the ogres of legend. It ran on its long sinewy arms, like the apes he'd seen in the jungles south of Cush.

But it was really a half-living and half-dead, decompos- ing mass of angry flesh and bone. The thing's scent could attest to that. It wore the stink of death like a cloak. Large, gaseous blisters swelled from the green skin covering most of its enormous body. With each movement, blisters burst, spewing out noxious fumes and leaving large portions of skin shredded and useless, as the creature lumbered toward him.

Skilurus rarely complained about the gift bestowed upon him by his heritage. As a hunter and tracker, the 'wolf' in him made for an excellent companion...even if he was unable to truly transform since his cloak had been destroyed by Ursus when they'd first met. But now, near this foul beast, his heightened sense of smell was becoming a burden. He was nearly overcome by the impulse to vomit the meager meal he'd eaten earlier in the day. But he dared not stop to ease his roiling stomach. The slightest misstep...the briefest of pauses...would result in the most gruesome of deaths. He would just have to endure.

He turned a corner, grabbing hold of a fence post to help swing him around, and then slammed into something short and squishy. The impact sent him tumbling head over foot, slurping through wet earth, the large creature only a few feet behind him. The moment he came to a stop, Skilurus sprang to his feet, and bolted forward again, only to be brought back down by something clinging to his ankle.

With a panicked scream, he shook his leg, trying to free himself from whatever was clutching it. The sole of his boot struck something hard. It was followed by a grunt of pain and then freedom. He leapt to his feet just as the lumbering beast rounded the corner. He was preparing to resume his run when he glanced down to see a bundle of fur rustling helplessly on the ground. The bundle whined. Or was it crying?

The ogre was now only a few strides away, but its writhing worm-filled mouth seemed to have lost interest in Skilurus. Instead, its massive head stared down at the crying cluster of furs.

Curious, Skilurus reached down and flipped the furs aside. Underneath, lying flat on the ground, was a little girl—no more than six years old.

She had been what Skilurus had stumbled over. She had grabbed hold of his ankle in a desperate attempt at salvation. He'd kicked her in the face to free himself.

And she is about to be stomped on by the brute's heel!

Before the ogre's foot came crashing down, the young man scooped the girl into his arms, and ran even faster than he had before. The stakes had never been higher. There was now a survivor to this massacre. An innocent young child. If Skilurus stumbled...if he slowed even for a second, it wouldn't just be his life that was forfeit. It would be the end of this scared little child as well. He would not allow that to happen.

The beast screamed in rage, then the sound of its lumbering footfalls splashed through the muck behind them. The girl cupped her ears with her hands and nestled deeper into Skilurus's chest as he ran. He had to do something. He had to end this chase, and fast. His heritage allowed him a certain level of endurance far beyond normal men, but there were limits even for him.

"Shhhhhh," he whispered into the child's ear as he ran. "Everything is going to be fine."

The girl shook in response, now sobbing into his cloak. He risked a quick glance back to see the ogre-thing gaining on them. It was now only about ten yards away, raising its giant fist above its head.

Without thinking, Skilurus skidded to a stop and leaned backward, allowing his momentum to carry his feet out from under him. He slid through the mud on his back. The creature, not expecting the move, released its fist into a mighty swing, propelling it forward and over the supine forms of its prey. It stumbled forward, just as the young man and his charge slid to a halt. The creature, unable to counter its foe's agile move, careened headfirst into a row of smoldering huts, fanning the embers as it passed. The embers struck unburned timber and burst into a new blaze.

Not waiting around to see what would happen next, Skilurus scrambled to his feet, repositioned the child against his chest and ran in the opposite direction.

Toward the sound of battle on the other side of the village.

Toward Ursus Rex.

King slammed his shield into a goblin's snout just before leapfrogging over its head and swinging his sword at his next attacker. The short Grecian blade—a relic he'd held onto since he first arrived in the past—sliced through the creature's neck, cutting clean through the spine. The goblin's head tipped from its shoulders, rolling to a stop at the feet of one of its companions. As the rest of the body hit the ground, a veritable tidal wave of inch-long worms poured from its open neck and wriggled away from the fight.

King squashed the fleeing maggots before they could get too far away, but there were still two of the goblin-Sluagh left—though one of them now boasted a pancaked face, thanks to King's shield. While the creatures excelled at overwhelming their foes through sheer numbers and brutality, they were little more than mindless drones with an instinct for killing.

An instinct, but fortunately not skill, King thought, as the uninjured Sluagh lashed out with its tentacle-like tongue. Sidestepping the attack, King withdrew a dagger from within his tunic, and hurled it toward the creature's mouth. The blade, perfectly balanced after the last few months over a blacksmith's kiln, flew past the writhing teeth-like worms inside the creature's mouth and skewered the back of its head with a disgusting *squish*.

King spun around to face the last of the decomposing monsters. The goblin was hunched down and shifting from one foot to another. Its gray, cloudy eyes burned at him with an insatiable hunger.

Or is that hatred?

"Can you understand me?" Curiosity had gotten the better of King. Since hearing about the trail of carnage these creatures had been leaving in their wake, he and the bishop had been debating their nature. Polycarp believed they were fueled by the demonic forces of hell itself, and therefore, were filled with malevolent intelligence. King, on the other hand, had argued that the Sluagh would eventually be explained away by natural means. A parasite maybe. Or a fungus similar to the type discovered in his own time that could manipulate ants to do its bidding. Simply put, he believed them to be driven by a Darwinian desire to survive. But the look in this goblin's eyes shook his confidence in the theory. There was just something menacing about them that went far beyond that of a mere animal. "We don't have to do this. Don't have to fight. If you understand me, speak. Maybe we can..."

Without telegraphing the move, the flat-nosed Sluagh spat out a serpentine rope of intertwining worms, six inches in diameter. Before King could react, the tongue's barbs embedded themselves into his neck, just above the cravat tucked down into his armor. He reacted without thought, grabbing the tentacle and ripping it from his throat. But not before the wriggling forms of at least three of them slithered under his skin.

Unsure of the effect that four of the worms would do to his near immortal body, a sudden flare of rage boiled up within his gut. With a berserker roar, he bolted directly for the creature with his sword held high in the air. The moment he came within two feet of it, however, something shot out from the alleyway to his right, slamming into him with a shout of surprise. King flew to the ground, entangled by the mass of arms and legs that had struck him. He rolled end over end. The moment he came to a stop, he slipped free and leapt to his feet in a defensive stance, but the Sluagh goblin was nowhere to be seen.

7

"Shit!" King spun around and glared down at Skilurus, who was just climbing to his feet. "I had it. What were you thinking?"

The young man was cradling something within his cloak, but King couldn't make out what it was. With one hand, Skilurus dusted his knees off and gave him an apologetic shrug. "I am sorry, my lord. But I was having problems of my own." He gently pulled his cloak aside to reveal the blood-smeared face of a young girl of about six years old. "Are you alright?" Skilurus asked the child. "Our tumble did not hurt you, did it?"

The girl, her eyes fixed warily on King, shook her head.

Skilurus smiled. "Good." He turned back to King. "I found her on the other side of the village while being chased...um...well, being chased by something. As far as I can tell, she is the only survivor."

King stepped forward, his eyes narrowing as he gazed into the young girl's eyes. "Are you sure?"

The young man cocked his head to one side. "Sure? About what?"

"That she *is* a survivor?"

Skilurus seemed to ponder that a moment, then his eyes widened in understanding. "Oh!" He glanced down at the child, then back at King. "She...she looks normal enough."

King gave the child a closer look. "Whatever these Sluagh do to reanimate bodies, it looks like they go through some pretty serious changes in a short amount of time. If she was one of them, she would show signs by now. And I see none."

The young man looked relieved.

"Now, where's the priest?" King asked.

"I am not sure. I left him with that man we found. Is he really Longinus? Have we truly found him after all this time?"

"You left the Padre *alone* with that thing?"

"He was saving our lives," a voice behind him said.

King turned to see Polycarp, with the man, Longinus, draped over one of the bishop's shoulders. They staggered toward him.

"Young Skilurus led one of the more daunting monsters on a merry chase, providing enough time for me to find a place for our ill friend here to hide until it was safe." The bishop turned to the young man and offered a nod of approval, as Skilurus sat the child on the ground near King. Then the young man dashed over to assist with Longinus. "Thank you, my boy. You are proving to be most surprising."

Skilurus beamed at the praise before gently helping Longinus to the ground.

King pondered the boy's actions for a moment and found no wrong in them. He motioned to Longinus and the child. "We need plans, for both of them."

But the old priest was no longer paying any attention to him. Instead, he moved to the girl, and was now whispering in her ear. The girl beamed and giggled at whatever the rotund man was saying to her, then whispered back. Her smile brightened, and she wrapped her arms around Polycarp's neck in an intense bear hug. After a moment, he kissed her on the forehead and turned back to King.

"Little Clarese here will be no trouble at all," Polycarp smiled. "She will be coming with us."

King glared at him. "You can't be serious. She'll get in our way."

The bishop cocked his head curiously. "Interesting."

"What is?"

Polycarp gently brushed a strand of hair from the girl's eyes as he looked up at King. "Something tells me you have not always been this callous toward the plight of those in need."

"It's not callousness. I've got no problem getting her out of this hell pit. Placing her with a loving family who'll take care of her. But we don't know what we're going to do with Longinus yet. Every minute she spends in his company—whatever his association with the Sluagh might be—is tantamount to her murder. You're calling me callous?"

"Trust me, Ursus." The old man laughed. "There is no safer place for this young one to be than with us."

King threw up his hands. "Then she's your responsibility. She dies, it's on your head."

Polycarp's face grew solemn, and he acknowledged the comment with a nod of his head.

"So, what now?" Skilurus asked, kneeling beside Longinus and applying a damp cloth across his brow. "We finally have him. Is it over?"

"I fear not." The bishop shook his head. "Though the scourge does still reside within him, I am afraid that something is not quite right. The sensations I am getting are not quite the same as when I first encountered him. It is different somehow. Weaker, yet more malevolent. I am not sure what it means." He paused, then glanced at King. His eyes narrowed. "What about you, Ursus? How do you fare after your battle?"

King reached up to his neck where the three worms had burrowed in. The fourth maggot digging into his leg also flashed through his mind. But the injuries had already healed. So far, there'd been no ill-effects. "They were faster than those I've fought in the past. Tougher to kill. But dumb as a slab of stone."

"You misunderstand. I meant, were you infected?"

He thought about that for a moment, then shook his head. "I don't think so. My body has a way of killing off any foreign parasites or illnesses that come my way."

"And you would do well to remember that we are not just dealing with a physical menace here, dear Ursus, but something far more sinister. Something both from the material *and* spiritual realms." Polycarp sighed. "So, I am assuming some of the creatures managed to latch their foul tongues onto you?"

King nodded.

"Then we must wait and see what transpires, and hope that much lauded healing ability of yours holds true." He bowed his head for a brief moment, before looking back up. "Or pray that He who is greater by far would intervene on your behalf."

The woman, cloaked in a shroud of mud, twigs and leaves, crouched in the charred branches of an oak tree, just outside the city walls. Her bright green eyes soaked in the three strangers, taking in every detail and committing them to memory.

Her rage seethed as she watched them bicker back and forth. The palms of her hands burned where she'd been gripping her bow too tightly for too long. The sweet, acrid stench of her charred people wafted up to her nose. Tears rolled down her cheeks, streaking the earthen camouflage she'd improvised.

She wasn't entirely certain what had happened. She'd left the village five days ago, to visit kin on the far side of the forest. The first sign of trouble she'd come across on the journey home was the grotesque desecration of her village's burial mound. Then, she'd seen the smoke rising.

By the time she'd made it to the nearly ruined village wall, it was all over. The three strangers had been huddled together in a heated discussion. From a distance, the woman could understand little of what they said. But she had no doubt that these men—including the Roman soldier who seemed to be the trio's leader—were responsible for the massacre that had taken the lives of everyone she held dear.

And she would have her revenge. She would make these monsters pay for what they...

Clarese?

The woman had been so engrossed by the strangers' exchange, she'd failed to see the child huddled in rags and cradled in the fat man's arms. The poor girl was covered in grime and viscera, but she could just make out the whites of her teeth. *Is she laughing? Surely not.*

But she couldn't deny it when the sound of giggles echoed up to her in the safety of the tree's branches. The child was indeed laughing. It wasn't her normal, belly-roll laugh that was so characteristic of Clarese, but it was there nonetheless. There was a hint of deep sadness and fear in it, but it was genuine and warm as well.

A mournful groan pulled her attention away from the little girl, and she turned her eyes toward the bedraggled man lying on the ground, clutching his abdomen as if his entrails were falling out. She didn't recognize him either. He wore the tattered rags of a beggar. Hardly a warrior. Definitely not someone she would need to concern herself with when it came time to free Clarese from whatever these men had planned for her.

The Roman stooped down near the beggar and scooped him into his arms. Then the trio began making their way to their horses at the city gates. They were leaving. Her time was running out. She'd have to make her move now if she had any hope of avenging her people.

With a single motion, she drew an arrow from the quiver strapped to her back, then nocked it before pulling back the string. She then lined up her target—the Roman, just as he placed his plumed helmet atop his head—and she took a deep breath to steady her aim. She was about to release when Clarese let out a boisterous laugh at something the fat man whispered in her ear.

The woman eased the bow back and sighed.

Something was not quite right. Clarese was a special child. An orphan whose parents had died two years before. The entire village had taken to raising her together. She was smart. Wise beyond her years. And a great judge of character. There was no way she'd be so at ease with these men if they were responsible for the devastation that had laid waste to their village.

Still, the woman was not quite ready to trust them. She would delay her vengeance for now, but she would follow them, keep a close eye on the child and discover more about these strangers. However, should they betray the young girl's trust...should they harm her in any way...there would be hell to pay. She would see to that personally.

8

King brought his horse to a stop before the fortified gate at Isca Silurum and signaled for his companions to do the same. The Second Legion of Augusta's great fortress had been a steadfast refuge to the citizens of Rome since Claudius had invaded Britannia sixty years earlier.

They had found their way here while tracking strange impressions in the ground from the village of Celwyn. The criss-crossing, serpentine grooves in the dirt had first been identified by Skilurus within a mile of the village. They'd been so alien to all of them that there'd been little doubt as to their origins.

The Sluagh.

But unlike any Sluagh they'd ever seen. They had to follow the trail and see where it led. Two days later, the trio, along with the still-unwell Longinus and Clarese, had found themselves on the fortress's outskirts. Travel weary and needing to find someone to look after Clarese, they all agreed to seek shelter among the famed Roman Legion.

Once within fifty yards of the gates, King raised up his right fist. "Hail! Watchman! Centurion Ursus Rex and his companions wish entry into your settlement." The fortress, which sat atop a steep embankment, was too high to see any of the guards stationed on the walls and watchtowers, but King knew they were there. He waited a moment, but no answer came to his request. "I say, hail! I am Centurion Ursus Rex, on a mission from Emperor Hadrian himself. I seek refuge!"

After several more moments of silence, King walked up and examined the gate. It was secure. Nothing seemed amiss. Yet, there was no answer. A battlement containing one of the most battle-ready legions in Britannia, and no one was standing guard at the city gates.

"Something isn't right," he said, glancing back at his companions.

Polycarp stepped up to him. "I see no battle damage. No sign of attack."

"That's what troubles me. It's as if the entire settlement has been abandoned without a fight." King looked over at the priest. "Sense anything?"

The bishop shook his head. "But that only means there is nothing evil here *now*. I cannot say if a place has been tainted in the past."

"What about you, Skil?" King asked. "Care to sniff around the wall's perimeter? Keep an eye out for the tracks we lost a few miles back."

The Scythian nodded, only halfway containing the excited grin stretching up one side of his face. He handed Clarese over to Polycarp, patted her lightly on the head and then took off to the south at full speed.

"What do you think is going on?" the bishop asked, after Skilurus had disappeared around the corner of the wall. "This does not look like the work of the Sluagh to me."

"And yet, the Second Augusta Legion appears to have abandoned their post," King said. "Even if they'd deployed for some confrontation, they would have left a small crew here to watch over the settlement. And they would have been guarding the gate." He turned his attention to the girl, who had wrapped her arms around the bishop's legs. She stared back at King with wondrous eyes. He shot her a playful wink, then looked back at the horses where Longinus hung limply over the back of King's horse, which he'd named Rook. "We'll know more once Skilurus returns. For now, we better check on our prisoner."

"I think we should kill him and be done with it."

"Huh?" King turned back to Polycarp. "What did you say?"

The bishop shook his head. "I did not say anything." His eyes then narrowed. "What...what did you think I said?"

King shook his head. "I...I'm not sure."

Polycarp eyed him, as if contemplating how he should respond. Before he could decide however, the two were interrupted by a shout from Skilurus from some distance away.

"Stay here," King told the bishop. "Watch over Longinus and the girl."

Before the old man could protest, King dashed off toward Skilurus's voice. He rounded the corner and ran another hundred and fifty yards before he saw the boy crouching near the fortress wall. When he heard King's approach, Skilurus looked up and pointed to the ground. That was when King noticed the loose dirt piled up on two sides. As he strode closer, he could see an opening in the ground. A very large hole, twenty feet in diameter at the base of the wall. "A tunnel?"

"Looks that way." Skilurus stood up, arching his back to pop his vertebrae. "And I can smell them. The Sluagh. The tunnel was definitely made by them."

When they'd lost the creature's trail earlier, it had never occurred to King that the Sluagh might have burrowed underground. He'd never heard of them doing such a thing before. Though, the more he thought about it, he'd also never heard of them maintaining their cadaverous form this long before either. Usually, when the Sluagh reanimated their patchwork dead, it was said the effect only lasted a few hours at best. Then, the body would simply begin to break down from decomposition, as well as from its natural wear and tear. It was becoming quite clear to him that the creature—or creatures—they were currently hunting was like nothing that had been encountered before. At least not in the last century or so.

Then, there was the trail itself. He'd never seen tracks like these before. Multiple, long, curved impressions in the soil. The tracks were beveled in a singular direction, as if an entire brood of sidewinders had slithered in tandem over the terrain.

An image flashed through his mind. A writhing mass of heaving serpentine arms intertwined in an orgasmic pirouette. Tentacles, tipped with hundreds of tiny mouths, each with thousands of teeth, lashed toward his mind's eye. He did not flinch, though the vision seemed real. Visceral. He could smell their foul stench. Feel the fetid wave of air washing across his face with each wriggling appendage. Yet he found himself unable to move. Unable to speak. All he could do was watch the mesmerizing dance of those strange snake-like...

"Ursus?"

King looked up from the hole at the young Scythian, his trance broken. "Yeah?"

"I asked you if you wanted me to search the tunnel. See where it led."

He shook his head. "No need. I'm sure it leads inside. I also know what we'll find inside." He tried to wrap his mind around it. An entire regiment...slaughtered. The Second Augusta Legion wiped out in a single day. "We'll check the fort together, and come back for the Padre if there are any survivors who need assistance."

Skilurus nodded, "I will lead the way. I can see better in the dark than you." Not waiting for King's reply, the young man stepped into the tunnel. King gave a quick glance in the direction of Polycarp, the girl and Longinus. Then he drew his sword and followed Skilurus into the dark.

9

A hundred yards through the tunnel, Skilurus came to a sudden halt. The tunnel had been huge. Twenty feet around and easy enough to walk through. But now, the ceiling began to taper off. Its strangely smooth surface shrank, forcing them to crawl the remaining distance.

The good news was that the exit was just up ahead. He could see the waning light of dusk just a few feet away. But something wasn't right. The foul stench beyond hit him like a club to the stomach. Only, it wasn't merely the common stench of death. Nor was it the telltale stink of the Sluagh. This was something different.

Something worse.

"What's wrong?" Ursus asked from behind him. "Why did you stop?"

Skilurus hesitated. He was unsure how to describe his trepidation. He'd spent months working on gaining Ursus Rex's trust. Had worked so hard to get to the point where the centurion allowed him to run free, as his kin had—despite lacking the cloak of his ancestors. He wanted to ensure that the man he so respected would one day respect him as well. But to voice his concerns now stank of cowardice. He couldn't have that. At the same time, it was his duty to warn his companion of the dangers that lay before them.

"There is something up ahead," was all he could think to say.

"Um, yeah. I was kind of expecting that."

"Yes, but this is... There is something wrong here."

Ursus's response was silence.

"I cannot explain it, m'lord," Skilurus continued. "Whatever is up ahead is even more malevolent than what we encountered in Celwyn, if that is possible."

Ursus let out a low growl. "There is no choice. We need to investigate." He paused as if considering something. "But when you get to the tunnel's exit, stop. Let me go through first."

Giving a nod he knew Ursus couldn't see, he resumed his crawl toward the purple-orange light of dusk. Once he reached the edge of the tunnel, he stood close to the curved wall, and peered outside. It took a moment for his eyes to adjust—not to the dwindling light, but to the reality of what he was seeing.

The entire interior of the fortress was painted in a deep shade of red. The stone wall, normally a bland shade of gray, was coated in rich crimson, still dripping with gelatinous viscosity.

The tunnel opening was nearly shoulder level with the surface, making it difficult to get a better view without climbing out. But from his vantage point, he could see scattered body parts—human, dog, horse and livestock alike—torn asunder and strewn everywhere along the fortress's main courtyard. There was no noise—not even a breeze or a whistle of a bird. *When did I last hear a bird?* he wondered. *Not since the carrion birds haunting Celwyn.*

Skilurus jumped when a hand gripped his shoulder. He turned to see Ursus, grim faced, yet offering a compassionate glimmer in his eyes.

"I'll go first," he whispered. "Wait thirty seconds. If I'm not attacked, then follow."

"If something happens to you, you want me to stay here?" He shook his head. "No, m'lord. I cannot do that."

"I'll have a much more difficult time if I'm worried about keeping you safe. So, if I'm attacked, *stay here.*" He tightening his grip on Skilurus's shoulder. "Understand?"

Is he worried about my safety or whether I will turn on him, like the monster he thinks me to be?

"Do you understand me?"

Skilurus gave a curt nod, and watched as Ursus scrambled up the dirt embankment and out into the courtyard above. Once outside, the centurion stood to his full six feet, and looked around. His nose wrinkled in disgust, and then he strode away out of view.

Twenty-six, twenty-five, twenty-four...

Skilurus inhaled deeply, mentally calculating the various scents his sensitive nose was detecting. So much death out there. So many bodies—or body parts. The smell of sword oil, leather and tempered bronze. Dung. Lots and lots of dung from the various animals that had called the fortress their home. And of course, there were odors infinitely more foul carried on the wind.

The smells of unholy things.

He chuckled at the thought. *Unholy things.* Before traveling with Bishop Polycarp, such notions were as alien to him as the sweltering dry climes of Jerusalem had been when he'd first met his two companions. His people, the Neuri had always resided in the mountains of Scythia—a place that Ursus called the Carpathian Mountains. They'd always been a hardy people. Their religion, though rich with ritual and magic, had little concept of demons and evil. To them, the only evil in the world was the inability to hunt. To become lame and unable to run in the wild. Until he'd met the bishop, Skilurus had only the vaguest of ideas about 'unholy' things. Now, however, they had become all too commonplace.

Fifteen, fourteen, thirteen...

Skilurus pushed the thought aside and focused on the here and now. He hadn't seen or heard Ursus since he slipped from view, and that troubled him. The man had to know how worried he was. Surely, he would offer brief updates on his exploration. But then, why should he? Ursus Rex trusted Skilurus only slightly more than he did Longinus.

The boy could hardly blame him. If the legends his grandfather had taught him were true, it was not the first time his ancestors had encountered the centurion. Ursus—using a different name—had ridden into Neuri territory some two hundred and fifty years before. He'd been searching for a missing woman, a mother of six who'd been taken violently from her home in the dead of night. Ursus had tracked her down to a Neuri settlement near the bank of the Hypanis River. Unfortunately for him, he arrived on the annual night of the hunt...the one night of the year that Skilurus's people could shed the confines of their human prison and run wild, hunting whatever or whoever they dared.

And they had hunted Ursus.

He'd fought bravely. Had killed a large number in return, but in the end, their numbers simply overwhelmed him. A pack of fifty—the strongest of their kind—had torn him to shreds. They had ripped him apart as violently as the poor souls laying in the blood-soaked courtyard now. The story went that the chieftain and the elders of the village gnawed on the man's bones for days afterwards. To the amazement of Skilurus's people, somehow, the skin and muscle tissue grew back. Again, and again. Thinking this was a blessing from the Ancestors, the tribal leaders ate the rapidly growing meat all over again.

That continued for months.

Ten, nine, eight...

Becoming impatient, Skilurus peeked over the lip of the exit, but saw no sign of his companion.

Ursus, where are you?

The heel of his foot shook with impatience, as he looked left, then right.

The young man knew he really had nothing to worry about. If the story his grandfather had told him was true, there seemed to be nothing that could kill the *Bear King*. Of course, Ursus had denied the story when Skilurus had asked him about it—at least, he'd denied the part about being torn to pieces and continually gnawed on for months. He'd laughed it off, labeling the story an over-inflated tall tale.

He hadn't denied being alive back then, though.

Skilurus's grandfather didn't know the fates of the men who had eaten his flesh for months. All that was known was that one night, when the moon was black as a celestial sackcloth, the entire village disappeared without a trace. Neighboring villages told tales of the undying man wandering the snow-covered foothills thereafter, hunting every wolf he found. Then, one day, as suddenly as he had appeared, the sightings simply ceased.

Despite Ursus's denial of the story, he certainly did not trust Skilurus or his people very much. If even a quarter of the legend was true, however, the boy could certainly understand. However, the magical art of transforming into a wolf had long since been lost to his people. None of them could 'wolf out', as Ursus called it. Not anymore. Even with the assistance of their wolf-cloaks, they could only heighten their senses, agility and strength. A few could grow hair with it. Perhaps elongate their snouts, which was merely caused by spiritual memories of ancestors long dead. The undying centurion had nothing at all to fear from Skilurus, and he wished the man would realize that once and for all.

Three, two, one...

Not desiring to wait another second, Skilurus scrambled up the dirt embankment and crawled out into the open air of the courtyard. He stood up, his muscles tense, and he turned to take in the macabre sight all around him. Then he sniffed the air. Once. Twice. *There is that strange smell again.* Unlike anything he'd encountered before.

He turned, trying to locate the odor's source. Then he carefully stepped over thick pools of blood and human limbs, taking in the various crimson-stained stone structures that once housed nearly a thousand soldiers. The blacksmith's hut now sat in smoldering ash; only a few wisps of smoke curled into the air from the embers. A single arm, ripped off at the elbow, hung off the top of the anvil—a hammer still clutched in its hand.

"Ursus?" Skilurus called in a hushed voice. "Where are you?"

Only silence answered him.

He stepped closer to the center of the courtyard. The strange smell was even stronger now. Then he drew his sword from its scabbard and raised it in a defensive stance. He was now standing under a brick archway that bridged the upper levels of two buildings—a barracks and what looked like a hospital. The underbelly of the arch was shrouded by the setting sun, blanketing it in rich, dark shadows.

Where did Ursus go?

He clutched his sword tighter while taking deep, anxious breaths. Slowly, he took another step into the shadow of the arch when something hot and wet struck his shoulder. With a jump, he swatted at whatever had landed on him. When he pulled his hand away, his palm was painted in red.

Blood.

With a sudden understanding, he looked up at the arch and peered deep into the shadows. There was something up there. Something large and amorphous. Something moving with slow, jerky motions. He was just about to step backward and away from the arch when the thing dropped from its perch and lunged at Skilurus with a tangle of long, tentacle-like arms.

10

The thing that dropped to the ground was like nothing Skilurus had ever seen in his life. It was a creature that defied even the most mad of nightmares. It was little more than one gelatinous mass of human tissue and body parts—seven feet around and four feet high—bound together like the enormous jellyfish he'd seen bobbing near the beaches of Greece. Deep purple-red veins spider-webbed across thin, translucent skin as it undulated toward him.

He stared in terror at the thing, unable to move. His eyes were locked in paralytic awe as he absorbed the monster's every detail. The creature moved along the ground in a way similar to a slug. It slowly inched itself forward along a flattened belly with a thick stream of clear viscous fluid trailing behind it. All around the creature's amorphous mass were dozens of long, rope-like arms that whipped through the air as it propelled itself forward. Atop the creature's form—Skilurus really couldn't call it a head—rested nearly two dozen, cloudy human eyes. Though none had eyelids, they seemed to glare at the boy with a vile hatred as it slithered toward him.

Finally, after an indeterminable number of seconds, Skilurus found the strength to take a step back. Then another. He wanted to turn and run, but he knew better. Years of ancestral instincts told him that turning his back on a predator like this would be his undoing. His best defense was to keep the creature in clear view until he could figure out a way to vanquish it with minimal risk.

"You, my friend, are quite ugly," he said, taking his sword in both hands now and holding it up in a parrying position.

The creature oozed forward. Its eyes fixed directly on him, then it stopped. Skilurus held his breath, waiting to see what would happen next.

He didn't have to wait long.

The creature convulsed. Its body shriveled up as if its insides were being suctioned out with some invisible hose.

It lay dormant for several long seconds. Its eyes stared blankly overhead, and its form sagged along its midsection.

Is it dead? Skilurus chided himself for such a stupid question. *Of course, it is, you imbecile. The creature is composed of nothing but the body parts of the dead. It was never really alive to begin...*

SHROOSH!

Before he could finish the thought, the thing shuddered, then swelled to twice its original size. A moment later, the creature burst open, releasing a fetid haze of olive green gas into the air. The gas's odor matched what he'd been sensing since entering the tunnel a few minutes before. Only now, it was much fouler. Stronger. And somehow, Skilurus knew, it was very toxic.

He dodged the gaseous miasma by leaping to the right. As he flew through the air, something hot and sticky latched on to his ankle, pulling him down to the blood-drenched soil. The impact flung the sword from his hand, and before he could recover it, he was yanked backward.

Toward the monster.

Toward his inevitable doom.

He twisted around, his ankle elevated above his head. One of the creature's tentacles was wrapped around his leg, pulling him into the air. As he was dragged up, a sharp sting ripped at his leg, like hundreds of tiny needles had begun puncturing him at once. Skilurus glanced at the tentacle's tip. Dozens of nearly imperceptible mouths, filled with sharp tiny teeth, coated the appendage. They gnawed at his flesh, and as a burning sensation flowed up his leg, he knew the creature's venom would soon render him helpless.

Although he'd dropped his sword, he was not without his assortment of other weapons. His hands fumbled in the fabric of his cloak, searching for a stash of knives he kept bound inside an interior pocket. Slipping one of the knives out, he attempted to lash out at the tentacle around his leg, but he was jerked as the creature dodged the attack. He tried again and again, but each time, the thing's appendage swung out of his reach.

He glanced down at the thing, which seemed to be entertained by his attempts to free himself, and hurled the knife straight down at the creature with all his strength. But the blade simply sliced into the decomposing blob of flesh and embedded itself harmlessly in its center mass. The attempt, however, was not without consequences. The tentacles' mouths renewed their assault on his ankle, which blossomed with agony as hundreds of needle-sharp teeth pierced his flesh.

His vision began to darken, as though the night's arrival had been sped up. The world around Skilurus spun out of control, and the young man found himself becoming drowsier with each tiny bite.

"The eyes!" someone shouted from what seemed like leagues away. It was a female voice. A decidedly lovely female voice. Like the song of angels—though Polycarp would certainly have rebuked him for asserting that angels were capable of singing. "Aim for the creature's eyes!"

The voice spoke in Latin, but with a strange accent Skilurus couldn't place. It was lilted with a sing-song cadence that would surely lull any savage beast to sleep. He twisted himself around, looking for the voice's source. But his mind was already addled by the poison coursing through his system. It was all he could do to keep his eyes open, much less search for the owner of such a melodic voice.

"I cannot get a clear shot!" the female shouted. "You are either going to have to do it, or you need to move!"

Skilurus wriggled his body, pulling his torso higher into the air until he was able to grab hold of the tentacle wrapped around his ankle.

Thwip! Thwip! Thwip!

The sound of three arrows whizzing through the air rang out just past his left ear, followed by a horrendous scream of rage and pain from below. Skilurus attempted to look down at the beast, but he found himself hurtling toward the ground before he could twist his body around. Just before he struck the earth, he caught a glimpse of three wooden shafts jutting up from the creature's human eyes.

Upon impact with the ground, Skilurus rolled to his left, sweeping up his sword and leaping back toward the tentacled beast. Before it could recover, he delivered a series of sweeping blows to the hulking mass. Blood and viscera spewed through the air as each sword thrust ripped through rotting flesh with sickening wet slaps. He screamed as his sword cut flaccid meat, over and over. Air-stifling panic, revulsion and rage coursed through the boy's veins, fueling his powerful swings in a whirlwind of rampant carnage. The creature's arms flailed about, trying desperately to counter the savage attack, but soon, one by one, each tentacle flopped to the ground in a putrid, bloody tangle. A twitch. A wiggle. Then nothing, except the inertial motion of a dead thing being hacked to pieces with the Scythian's curved blade.

A gentle hand touched Skilurus's shoulder, breaking the trance-like fury of his attack, and sending him into an altogether new panic. With a jump, he swung around, ready to bring his sword down on this new presence. But his blade was easily blocked by a sturdy, ash bow.

11

Skilurus stared dumbfounded at the beautiful, dark-haired woman, whose bow pushed his sword to the side. Her face was mottled with dirt and grime, but through the filth, he could see the outline of her fine chin, plump lips and bright sky-blue eyes. Her long slender neck cocked to one side as she stared back at him with one side of her supple lips curving up in a confident grin.

"Are you going to lower that sword, or am I going to have to take my bow to the side of your head?" she whispered.

The lad continued his open-mouthed stare for several more moments, trying to process this stranger's presence in such a dark and unexpected place. His brain was encumbered by the sweet lilt of her words—like honey dripping from a comb.

"Er, laddie? Are you listening to me?"

Her words broke through his mental wall of haze. He shook his head to clear his thoughts, and then lowered his sword. "Sorry about that." He looked over at the hacked up carcass of the monster he'd just killed. "I was a little distracted."

"I can see that." Her smile broadened and she slipped her bow across her back.

"Thank you. For your assistance, I mean."

She nodded, then took him by the hand and pulled him back toward the tunnel. "Come on. We need to leave this place. Now. Evil haunts these walls. This is no place for the living."

Skilurus shrugged out of her grip. "Wait. I cannot leave yet."

The woman glanced back at him, then at the dead creature laying a few feet away. "We do not have the time to argue about this. There are more of those things lurking about. That, you can be sure of. We need to go."

"Not without Ursus. I cannot leave him!"

"Your friend is as good as dead, lad. Trust me. I have seen what these foul things can do." She took hold of his forearm. "Saw what they did to my village. You are lucky to have survived with your own skin. I doubt this Ursus fellow fared better if he was alone."

"Who are you?" Skilurus growled, pulling away from her again, sweat pouring down his head from the venom coursing through his blood. "Why are you trying so hard to get me to leave this place?"

"I am trying to protect you, oaf!"

"But...why? I do not know you. And you do not know me. So why risk your life by helping me?"

"Because..." She paused, glancing down at her feet. "...I watched you with Clarese. Saw you protect her. Carry her to safety, despite the risk to yourself. I owe you for that, and I aim to pay you back."

"You know Clarese?"

She nodded. "I am her guardian. Her protector. I had been visiting a nearby village. When I returned home, I saw the smoke. The devastation. Thought everything was lost. Until that is, I saw Clarese in your care."

Skilurus scratched at his sweaty scalp as he pondered her words. "But she is a little girl. What does she need a protector for?"

"Clarese is not an ordinary girl," the woman said. "She is a Druid priestess. Maybe the most powerful Druid to ever live, in fact. She was our healer, too. Her parents died of the fever a few years ago. The chieftain asked me to look after her ever since. To guide her and help her improve her skills of healing." She shrugged with a sigh. "It has not been easy, either. The wee one never speaks. She learns. She heals. She ministers. But she never voices her concerns or fears, making it hard to..."

"What are you talking about? She speaks. She has been talking to the priest ever since meeting him," Skilurus said.

The woman shook her head. "Impossible. For as long as I have known her, she has not uttered a single word."

"Um, if that is true, then how did Polycarp know her name was Clarese? She told him her name before we had even left your village."

"But that is imposs..."

A horrific scream erupted from somewhere in the center of the fortress, cutting off their conversation.

"Come on!" The woman took hold of Skilurus's cloak and dragged him toward the tunnel. "We wasted too much time!"

Another scream. This time longer, more pronounced. And unmistakably human.

"That is Ursus!" Skilurus shouted, pulling away for a third time and darting toward the sound.

"Wait!" He could hear her running after him, but he didn't slow down. Instead, the Neuri rounded the next corner and ran straight for Caesar Augustus's temple, for whom the Legion was named.

"You cannot go in there!" the dark-haired beauty shouted.

But he didn't listen. He skidded to a halt at the great wooden doors leading into the temple. The doors were still slightly ajar. A swath of blood—still wet and dripping—coated the ringed handles.

"You do not know if that is your friend's blood." The woman was now standing directly behind him. "He might have safely returned to the others."

Skilurus knew she didn't believe that. The blood was just too fresh. But there was one way he could be sure. He leaned into the door, taking three quick sniffs, and then he reeled back.

The scent was Ursus Rex's, but different.

Tainted.

Fearing the worst, yet unwilling to give his companion up for dead, he turned to the woman and held out his sword. "Take this," he said. "I will not be able to use it while doing what I am about to do."

Tentatively, she took the sword. "What exactly are you..."

But before she could finish the question, he'd stripped out of his tunic, dropped to all fours and bounded through the open door.

The air within the temple was foul, assaulting Skilurus's heightened senses with every breath. The rough-hewn stone walls of the temple corridor were lined with torches. Some were lit, producing a dancing miasma of shadow and light for him to see by. The rest hung useless within their sconces, creating long stretches of darkness in which any number of vile monsters could be lurking. The bitter-sweet tang of blood, mingled with the putrefaction of an untold number of human corpses piled along the corridor, made it difficult for him to concentrate. But he pushed his rising nausea away and struggled to target the one scent he most wanted to find—Ursus. Within less than a minute, he'd found it, and he began navigating the hallway toward the inner sanctum of the temple at a brisk, but stealthy pace.

Though he hadn't really expected anything different, the strange woman had apparently not followed him, and Skilurus wasn't sure whether he was thankful for that or disappointed. Her bow would have been valuable. And he now regretted giving up his sword to her so he could maximize his maneuverability and stealth. He'd not grown claws nor fangs since Ursus had burned his wolf pelt, and he now realized he was heading, unarmed, into the bowels of the bishop's hell.

Still, despite the danger, he had no choice. His mentor and friend was now in danger. The man who'd saved him from—well, just saved him—needed him now more than ever, and Skilurus would not let him down.

After creeping through the shadows a hundred and fifty feet from the entrance, he slowed and held his breath. He'd thought he heard something up ahead, but couldn't quite place it. He'd come to a point where there were no more lit torches, and the path ahead was black as pitch. His heritage provided him with above average night vision, but his eyes required time to adjust. A few moments later, the dark gave way to various shades of gray and Skilurus found that he could once again take in his surroundings.

There were no monsters hiding within the shadows. Merely fifty more yards of hallway leading directly to another large wooden door, leading to the temple's sanctuary.

He stepped forward. Then stepped again. Listening after each tentative footfall. Sniffing the air between every heartbeat. Ready to move should any ambush come. But the closer he came to the sanctuary, the more confident he became that no ambush was waiting for him. At least, not on this side of the door. But there was one thing he knew for certain. Ursus was on the other side as well. His scent was even stronger now. The peculiar odor from his blood, thicker. And now, he could discern quiet groans sliding through the door's thick oak planks.

Two more steps and Skilurus was at the door. He took in a deep breath, muttered a silent prayer to the gods of his people and put his shoulder into the door. It crept open, its rusted hinges creaking as it swung. Once there was room, he squeezed through the opening and found himself in an elaborate chamber, dripping with the blood and viscera of fallen legionnaires who once worshipped the Caesar in this very place.

By now, he was becoming accustomed to the sight of gore and limbs strewn wherever the Sluagh struck. The very thought unnerved him. What, after all, did it say about him that such carnage could mean so little after such a short period of time? But he put the thought out of his mind as he stepped over an arm, torn away from some poor soul's elbow. He looked around the sanctuary. There was little to see other than the devastation that had become all so familiar with these creatures. The stone walls were hardly visible beneath all the blood. The floors were cluttered with limbs, organs, human skin and more bones than Skilurus could count. He glanced up at the ceilings, where dark red ooze dripped into pools along the floors.

But there seemed to be no monsters lying in wait for him. No sign of Ursus either. He turned slowly, making a full three hundred and sixty degree sweep of the chamber. The only thing that remotely stood out as being unusual, besides the obvious carnage, was a mass of tissue hanging from the wooden rafters above him. The tissue was long and stringy, reminding Skilurus of human bowels. He focused on it. Willing his eyes to adjust further to the dimness, he gave the human garland a closer look.

That was when he saw something moving from within the bundle. A slight jerk, at first. Then, a tremble, followed by a sudden flurry of flailing amid the intestines. They weren't intestines at all, but rather tentacle-like worms. And they were clinging to something, squeezing a vaguely human-like form.

He stepped forward for a better look and gasped. Hanging from the rafters, wrapped in a cocoon of writhing tentacles, was Ursus. Deep lacerations and oozing sores covered the portions of his body still visible among the entwined appendages. But the tentacles weren't merely wrapped around the man. They had exploded *out* of him. His sores were everywhere, and out of each new orifice a different worm stretched out to the rafters. From Skilurus's vantage point, his mentor was not only caught in a web of elongated maggots, but he was the bridge that held them all together.

By the gods.

Ursus's face was contorted in a mask of unadulterated agony. His arms and legs thrashed in sickening spasms, yet from what Skilurus could tell, Ursus was unconscious and oblivious to the world around him.

Skilurus took a step forward, calculating the best way to cut his friend down, when he heard three low growls behind him. He spun around, just in time to see the creatures lowering themselves from the ceiling on cords of skin-like tissue—malformed, necrotic spiders. Before he could react, all three bounded toward him.

12

King wasn't sure where he was. He couldn't see. Couldn't move. Couldn't feel. But he could hear. Only, he wasn't certain the voices cursing at him were audible to anyone but him. And curse they did, screaming like angry drunks.

"You abandoned everyone you hold dear!" one of the voices shrieked.

"Left them!"

"Hurt them!"

"Tore out their hearts, you did!"

"It wasn't my fault!" he yelled back, but he knew his mouth—his vocal cords—were far too paralyzed to actually speak the words aloud. "I didn't want to..."

"They are going to die, you know."

"Your friends."

"Your team."

"Your precious Sara and Fiona."

The voices surrounded him. Entangled him. Like the tendrils of some great squid, the words coiled around him, and then cut deep into skin he could no longer feel.

"Because you are not there, they are going to die."

"Some, sooner than others."

"Because you abandoned them."

"Left them to fend for themselves."

King ground his teeth.

Or at least, he thought he did. For all he knew, he had no teeth to grind.

"Who are you? What are you?" he shouted. "What do you want with me?"

"You know..."

"...what we are."

"The priest told you."

"You're not demons."

"What makes you so sure?"

"Hmmm? Yes. What..."

"...makes you so certain?"

King shook his head. "Even if demons are real, they're spiritual beings. You..." He paused, trying to remember the events of the last few days. It seemed like centuries had gone by. The memories of Celwyn and the villagers massacred by the Sluagh were already fading. "You are the worms. The maggots. I don't know how, but somehow, you're...you're sentient."

"Are we?"

"I had no idea."

"We like being sentient."

"Never been sentient before."

"Perhaps..." This next voice was different than the rest. Calmer. More composed. With a distinct female voice. *"Perhaps, we are demons after all. Or maybe not. Perhaps your brain is simply trying to make sense of the changes we are making in your body."*

"No! We are sentient!"

"Sentient!"

"Yes, sentient! We like being sentient!"

To King, the female's explanation contained a ring of truth to it. It made a lot more sense than the legends of a cadre of damned souls so evil they'd been kicked out of Hell. And though he couldn't entirely discount the existence of demons, he'd spent enough time in Sunday School as a kid to know they weren't of the physical world. At the same time, he also knew at this precise moment, suspended in an unknown world, he couldn't trust anything he was told.

"What do you want with me? Why are you doing this?" *Whatever* this *is?*

"We are playing!"

"We are feeding!"

"We are growing and..."

"So this is what you did to Longinus? You tortured him like this for nearly a hundred years?"

"Not like this," said the soothing female voice. *"We did not have to. His mind and body were already fractured when we found him. You, on the other hand..."*

"I'm different."

"Yes. Very, very different."

"I'm immortal."

There was a pause.

He felt the voices constrict tighter around his arms and chest. Felt them tighten around his neck and legs. He realized it was the first time he'd sensed the presence of his limbs since awakening in this pitch black hell. Was that a good thing or bad?

Keep them talking, Sigler. The more they talk, the more aware of my surroundings I become.

"Not quite," she said. *"But close enough. You have seen what we do with your dead, no?"*

"You harvest parts. Merge them together, then reanimate the whole."

"Precisely."

"Why?"

"Why not?"

"That's not an answer."

She laughed at that. *"Simple. We do it to get where we need to be. Legs, Jack Sigler. Arms. Legs. Ambulation. We need them for the Hunt. We need them for our journey and for the Hunt."*

King noticed the cadence of her words was beginning to waiver. It was less fluid. Choppier. More akin to the myriad insane voices pummeling at his soul.

"And me? What do you need with me?"

"We have never seen anyone like you before. The bodies we harvest degrade. Fall apart. Even a living person—like Centurion Longinus—will eventually die and wither and fade. No matter how much we mend his body back together. He will eventually die and decompose to uselessness."

"But I won't."

"Not for a very long time."

"So why haven't you done it already? Why haven't you taken full control of me the way you did Longinus?"

Silence. Not just the female voice. All of them had fallen into a deep hush.

"Answer me!" This time, his own words were audible. His physical ears had actually heard his cry. He'd not uttered words, though. Not even syllables. But his voice had been loud and mournful.

And still, there was nothing but silence all around him. "Talk to me!"

He was becoming frantic. Though he didn't know why, talking to these creatures had begun to chip away at the mental prison in which they'd placed him. But now, the silence. What would happen? Did they sense their mistake? Would he fall back into his catatonic state?

His heart raced.

A heartbeat. I have a heartbeat.

"No!" The female finally spoke, and she sounded panicked. *"He will ruin everything!"*

Is she talking about me?

"Do not worry…"

"…our Mother!"

"We will deal with this…"

"Interloper."

"This…"

"…mongrel."

Mongrel? That doesn't sound like they're talking about me. Sounds more like…

"Ursus!"

The voice sounded like it was a thousand miles away, but it was clear. Distinct. Familiar. And young. So very young.

He heard shouts and growls. Audibly. Not in his mind. His hearing was returning.

"Ursus, I am coming for you!"

Skilurus.

13

From the sound of it, Skilurus wasn't faring very well. Howls and screams echoed off stone walls around him. King knew that much. He could remember exploring the fortress. Recalled finding the entrance to Augustus Caesar's temple. The torches and stone walls. The oak doors and beamed rafters.

King felt his muscles tense. Felt his arms and legs flexing against wet, viscous bonds squeezing his limbs. Then, he opened his eyes. Only a sliver at first. Even in the dim light of the temple's inner sanctum, his vision burned. The little bit he *could* see was hazy. Ill-defined.

There was a blur of motion below him that caught his attention. He looked down to see four shadowy figures scurrying along the floor. Then he struggled to differentiate the players within the combative ballet, but his eyes just couldn't quite adjust.

Come on, Jack! He struggled against the bonds that held him in place. *Skilurus needs you.*

King continued to watch. His vision focused. The gray shapes gave way to identifiable forms. Skilurus was crouching just below him. He had no weapons that King could see. No means to defend himself. And three Sluagh beasts paced around him like a circling wagon train made of decomposing flesh.

"*Skjndk...*" King tried to call out to the boy, but his mouth couldn't form the words. Whatever the worms had done to him, his body was struggling to compensate.

One of the creatures—a cat-like beast of four and a half-feet tall on all fours—lunged toward Skilurus. The young man spun to the left and barely avoided the monster's six inch claws skewering him in the gut. But he was too late to dodge the squirming tentacles of a second creature, which lashed out at him with striking snake-like motions. The wormy tentacles wrapped around the boy's arms and legs, pulling him to the ground. Skilurus struggled to break free, but the worms' teeth had already latched on to his bare skin and wouldn't let go.

King strained against his bonds again, his muscle and skin tearing from the effort. He glanced down at his chest. The worm-tentacles writhed from the cavities they'd created along his body. They stretched themselves out to latch onto the wooden beams above him.

Desperate, with no weapons he could reach, King dipped his head and bit down on the closest worm he could find. The squirming thing burst as he crunched down with his teeth. Putrid goo exploded from the worm's body as he chewed away at it. A second later, he'd freed himself from one of the bonds.

Only several dozen more to go.

It was a grim thought. He was pretty sure that the larvae were toxic, but he had confidence in his ability to heal. Still, his immortality would do nothing for the horrid taste on his tongue. It was a small price to pay for freedom and for helping his young friend.

He found the next closest worm and chewed it away as well. Then another. He pulled his right arm close to his face, stretched out his head and tore at the worms attached to his wrist. Now, with one arm free, it was easier to wreak havoc on the foul creatures infesting him. He raised his right knee and ripped the tendrils from his ankle. Then he did the same with his left, until all that kept him suspended were the worms gripping his left arm. A moment later, he was falling to the dirt floor of the temple in a heap of half-gnawed tentacles, foul-smelling fluids and copious amounts of his own tainted blood.

"Ursus!" King heard Skilurus shout, but he couldn't tell from which direction it came. Or how far away. His body wasn't healing nearly as fast as it should, and he'd endured more physical trauma than he had in centuries. But for some reason, his near-immortal regenerative capabilities seemed sluggish. Blood continued to pour from each open wound created by the Sluagh worms. They weren't closing, and King wondered if the 'Mother' hadn't been bluffing when she'd suggested they were essentially rearranging his

DNA—making it more compatible a habitat in which they could live.

"Ursus, help!"

With great effort, King lifted his head, and tried to look around. His eyesight was still blurry, but at least the shapes in the room were coming more into focus with each second. He saw Skilurus a few feet away. The young man was flat on his back, and he looked ill. The cat-creature padded toward him, great streams of bile-like saliva glistening from its toothy maw. The other two Sluagh—sporting dozens of human eyes along their amorphous bodies—kept him immobile with powerful tentacles.

Skilurus had just seconds. King needed to act, but he couldn't push himself up off the ground. His limbs felt like they'd been filled with cement. He couldn't move.

"Skil, you need to wolf out!" he yelled. "Do it now!"

"I cannot! I have tried!"

The young Neuri was panicking. He was unable to gain enough focus to tap into his bestial instincts. And he was going to die because King was powerless to act.

Thwunk! Thwunk!

The sound of a bow caught King's attention just in time to see two arrows slam into the cat-creature. Craning his head, he looked toward the sound to see a slender, tattooed female standing just inside the sanctuary's giant wooden door. She nocked a third arrow, drew the bow string back and let it fly. The arrow's tip plunged straight into the cat-creature's left eye, eliciting a screeching howl from the undead thing.

"Boy!" she shouted. "Take your sword!"

Without waiting for him to respond, she slipped the blade out from her belt, and tossed it toward Skilurus. But the tentacled Sluagh tightened their hold on his wrists, preventing him from grabbing the weapon. The sword hit the ground, and slid to within inches of King's numb hands.

The newcomer's entrance did not go unnoticed. Two more decomposing creatures—very human in form—scurried headfirst down the sanctuary's stone walls, and then lunged for her. With a grace that only comes from years of training, the woman ducked and rolled to her right. The creatures, unable to compensate for her swift action, missed. Their momentum carried their legs forward, while their torsos twisted to reacquire their prey. As a result, the two monsters stumbled over each other, and fell to the ground in a tangle of limbs.

Taking advantage of their clumsiness, she withdrew a long, curved hunting knife strapped to her leg. She then set to work dismembering both of the patchwork creatures with the efficiency of a skilled butcher.

Damn. Don't know who this woman is, but I like her. Of course, he knew why. Her skill with a knife reminded him of his future teammate: Queen, a woman for whom he had tremendous respect.

The fingers of his right hand twitched at the thought. He shuddered to think how much Queen would ridicule him if she saw him flat on his ass, unable to move, while friends were in trouble. She'd never let him live it down.

He focused on his twitching fingers, and soon, he felt them flexing. Curling. His hand was beginning to make a fist. Once it was formed, he tightened it, feeling his strength return to his hand in a surge of will. Building on these small accomplishments, he placed both hands on the ground, and attempted to push himself up. After two tries, he found himself on his hands and knees, and reaching for the sword the newcomer had tossed to Skilurus. Since he wasn't sure where his own sword was, the kid's curved Scythian blade would have to do. With trembling fingers, he grabbed the sword's hilt, placed the blade on the ground, and used its strength to help himself stand up.

The world around him swayed left and right, and he struggled to stay upright. Although he'd lost a lot of blood, his wounds had finally healed. His strength would return soon enough, but he didn't have the time to wait. He'd have to do his best with what little strength he had left.

He only hoped it would be enough.

14

King leapt forward, swinging the blade down into the back of the cat-creature's neck. It bit deep, but didn't cut clean through, and the cat whipped its head around with a feral hiss, wrenching the hilt from King's weakened hands.

"You should not have done that," came the soothing female voice, deep inside King's head. *"You just made it angry."*

"Shut up." The words came out as little more than a growl, as he dove to his left just when the cat-thing attacked. When he hit the ground, he came up in a roll, spun around and yanked the sword from the creature's neck as it passed. Using the roll's momentum, he brought down the blade again, this time severing the cat's neck with a second swing.

The Sluagh's body flew to the ground and burst into its individual patchwork parts and a legion of white squiggling worms.

"Ursus!"

King watched as the larvae wriggled off into the shadows, then he turned toward Skilurus. The two tentacled creatures—giant, multi-eyed slugs made of human skin tissue—pulled the young man's arms in opposite directions. With their free tentacles, they lashed out at him. Their mouth-filled tips bit, scratched and tore at Skilurus's flesh with a hateful vengeance.

King prayed that the kid hadn't been infected with the Sluagh, like he'd been. He wasn't certain Skilurus would be able to last long against their influence, and he shuddered to think of what they might do with the wolf instinct within him.

Shoving these concerns aside, he bolted toward the monster on Skilurus's left, and swung his sword. But his target was much more agile than its slug-like body appeared. As the blade swept down, the creature shifted the brunt of its bulk toward its back, which swelled up like a crimped water hose. The front portion shrank and King's sword passed harmlessly overhead.

"Look out!"

Before King could heed the woman's warning, the second slug's tentacles wrapped around his neck. With a jerk, the powerful appendage hefted him off the ground, then slung him into a nearby stone wall.

The stranger unleashed three arrows, just as King scrambled back to his feet. Each arrow plunged deep into one of the slug's eyes, causing it to tremble and quake. Taking advantage of the creature's pain, he scooped up the sword and charged at full speed. The blade hacked into the injured slug, severing the thing in two. King then spun around, and thrust the sword at the second slug, driving the blade into its side, and filleting the top portion of the creature away from its lower half.

Satisfied that the thing was dead, King whirled around, looking for the next nightmare he'd have to slay. There were none to be found. He took a breath. Then two. Still nothing. Not even a sound, other than the heavy breaths of his companions.

"Are they...are they gone?" Skilurus asked, sitting up and checking himself over to ensure there were no serious injuries.

King was covered in blood, slime and other semi-liquids he would rather not think about, a task made difficult thanks to the foul stench permeating his skin, clothes and hair. But it appeared, for the moment, that they were alone in the old sanctuary of Augustus.

He gave a tentative nod. "Looks that way, Skil."

"No, Jack Sigler," came the feminine voice in his head. *"We are still here. We will always..."*

"Be here."

"Always."

"There is no getting rid of us."

"Ever."

The voices began a round of malicious laughter that only King could hear, but he ignored them as the strange tattooed female strode up to Skilurus and helped him to his feet.

"You came back," Skilurus said to her, squeezing her hand.

She shrugged. "My debt, it seems, is not quite paid, lad." She turned to King. "You..." She paused, looking him up and down appreciatively. "You are quite the warrior, Centurion."

"You have not seen anything," Skilurus said, smiling ear to ear. His cheeks were flushed as he looked at the dark-haired beauty. "Ursus is the greatest warrior of all time."

"Ursus?" She eyed King. "The bear?"

"Ursus Rex. The Bear King." Skilurus said. "A name bestowed on him by Caesar himself after he..."

"Skilurus," King interrupted. "Our friends are waiting outside. The Sluagh aren't defeated. They've just eluded us again. We need to get back on their trail."

King picked up his own sword, handed Skilurus's blade back to him and headed toward the sanctuary's doors. He was curious as to who the newcomer was and what she had to do with his rescue, but getting back to Polycarp was much more important. He had much to discuss with the old priest. Much to question him about concerning the voices that had taken up residence in his mind and the implications their presence had on his future. The Sluagh might not be demons, but they were definitely the closest thing a bio-logical entity could muster, and that meant the old man was his best bet with regard to getting rid of them. He'd just have to filter through the Christian mysticism to get to the real, scientific truth of the matter.

"Ursus is older than he looks, and speaks with strange words," Skilurus was telling the woman as they strode to the door. "Like when he calls Bishop Polycarp *Padre*'. I am not quite sure what that even..."

Before he could finish the sentence, the ground beneath their feet shook with a force that brought all three of them to their knees.

"What is happening?" Skilurus shouted above the din.

The dirt floor underneath shifted and split, as the rumbling grew stronger. Chunks of stone rained down from the walls and ceiling, nearly crushing them.

"Quick!" King shouted, scrambling to the door and pulling it open. "Beneath the threshold!"

His two companions obeyed and huddled beside him underneath the great oaken doorframe. King wasn't certain whether it would hold under the strain, but the support beams on either side of the large doors were safer than anywhere else within the temple.

The three watched as the fissure in the middle of the sanctuary grew wider, then burst open, sprouting hundreds of tentacles, each the width of an average human thigh.

"Um, Ursus?"

"I see them." King gripped the hilt of his sword.

The enormous creature lumbered up out of the cracking soil like a sperm whale cresting for a breath of air. But the monster didn't resemble any aquatic mammal King had ever seen. Though it hadn't yet fully emerged, the thing was easily twenty-five yards across and twice as long, with three-foot-long, sharp spines jutting up from its back. The creature's tentacles sprouted randomly from its entire body. Some thick and stubby. Others wispy and long. All containing hundreds of tooth-filled mouths that snapped at the air with a ravenous appetite. Like all the other Sluagh creatures, this one was composed of patchwork pieces of the humans and animals it had slaughtered, which made its head all the more macabre. At least, King assumed it was the head, because it was covered by the agonized faces ripped straight from the skulls of dozens of its human victims. Their mouths and eyelids stretched wide in terror and accusation, patched hodgepodge across the front of the beast's body, as it pulled its enormous girth out of the ground with a rumbling groan.

"I can honestly say, I did *not* see that coming," King said. His voice was almost a whisper. "Okay. When I say so, run. Get the hell out of here as fast as you..."

King's words trailed off as the creature shifted its weight and turned its massive head toward the door. The thing gave a quick shudder, then the patched-up faces began to twitch and writhe with each of the beast's movements. The sight was unsettling, to say the least. Twenty-four disembodied faces scowled at the trio under the doorway, as if they were still alive.

The faces shifted, twisting around the beast's head until a single soft face positioned itself in the center. Unlike the rest, this one had yet to see any signs of decomposition. To distinguish it further, it was unmistakably female.

"Go," King said with a clear, steady voice.

His companions, however, didn't move. They simply continued to stare as the monster shifted again, making its voluminous body ripple in waves.

But the central face—the woman's face in the center of the creature's forehead—was no longer shaking. Instead, it stretched away from the rest of the body, slowly oozing out of the bloated thing, like a foal being birthed. Within seconds, where there had only been a flat, two-dimensional face stitched onto the creature's hide, now there was the sleek feminine form of a beautiful woman hovering two feet off the ground.

King gazed at her naked form, and noticed the appendage jutting out from the back of her skull. It curved high into the air before folding back into the mass of the creature's body. The 'woman' was merely a tentacle given form, like a lascivious lure on an earthbound angler fish.

"Ursus?" Skilurus's voice sounded far away, but King knew the young man was still huddled inside the doorframe along with the archer.

"I said, 'go'. I'll be right behind you."

But King knew that was a lie. The angler fish lure was for him. He knew what she wanted. And before he was aware of it, he dropped his sword to the ground and moved toward her outstretched arms against his will.

15

"Yes, Jack," the woman said to him. Her voice, in his head, matched the one he'd heard before. He gave a quick glance back at Skilurus and the stranger, who still had not obeyed his command to run. They had not heard the voice. *"Now, you are merely a son of Adam, but we will make you into much more. We will make you into a son of Cain."*

The phrases were familiar to King. Biblical references? Fragments of felt-board lessons from his Sunday School teacher, Mrs. Montgomery, flashed through his mind's eye. Or was it Polycarp?

Cain.

According to the Bible, the world's first murderer. His motive? Envy. His punishment? To wander the earth, marked by a sign of God. For centuries, all sorts of speculation had been offered regarding what that mark was, but no concrete answer had ever been discovered. The story explained that the mark was passed down through all of Cain's line. His lineage was cursed, it was said, for all time. So any 'Son of Cain' would inherit the curse.

So does that mean the Sluagh are the 'mark'?

"Ursus, what are you doing?" Skilurus asked.

King ignored the question, stepping closer to the woman. Unable to pull his eyes away from her, he struggled to capture her ethereal beauty. It was beyond any mortal's understanding and impossible to describe. Though her form carried a feminine grace that drew his eyes, it was her face that was most difficult to connect with. It seemed to shimmer and shift in waves, like a rippling current in a pond. Slender and full-lipped one second, plumper with high cheekbones the next. She carried not just one face, but several that flashed and shifted with the shadows and light. And each of them was lovely beyond anything he'd ever seen before.

"I could be yours," the thing said. The voice was no longer in his head. It was spoken. Audible. But it sounded

as if spoken from several sultry voices all at once. *"For all eternity."*

He stopped right in front of her. Her arms stretched around his shoulders and pulled him against her in a lover's embrace. Her hands ran through his unkempt hair and traced the outline of his beard down his cheeks. She lifted his chin and looked into his eyes, and her face beamed with love and familiarity.

"Sara," King whispered, as something deep inside him cracked.

"Ursus!" Skilurus's shout was frantic now, but King hardly heard it.

"Our embrace will become legendary, my love. Our offspring will be like gods!"

Offspring?

The single word struck King like an open-palmed slap to the face.

She's a lure, Sigler. Remember. Anglerfish. She's not real. Not Sara.

But the more clarity he managed to obtain, the tighter the embrace became, until something hot and sharp pierced the base of his neck. A moment later, he could feel a wriggling wave of larvae washing down over his back. He could hear the worms' flat bodies striking the hard earth at his feet. Smell the pungent stingy whiff of ammonia wafting up to his nose.

"Yes, my love. Behold, your children! Each imbued with your wondrous gift of near-immortality. Each capable of sustaining the life of its host indefinitely."

King glanced down at his feet and couldn't contain a shudder, as a river of gray-white maggots—in numbers greater than he could imagine—undulated their way past the ephemeral beauty and toward the giant, tentacled beast behind her. The creature opened its mouth, reminding King of a pustulating knife wound, and the larvae horde wiggled their way inside.

"I...I..." King tried to protest, but the words wouldn't come. Or rather, he couldn't find enough air in his lungs to vocalize them. Deprived of oxygen, he struggled to push away from her embrace, but his strength was already waning.

"Shhhhh, sweet Jack. Just relax." Her voice was back inside his mind. *"You know as well as I that you cannot die from suffocation. No, we have much bigger plans for you than simply killing you."*

Stop it, he thought. *You're not real. You're not intelligent. Just a parasite. My mind is creating this conversation. My subconscious.*

"And what are the parasites doing, my love?"

What you always do. Harvesting DNA. Transforming it. Reshaping it. Molding it into a means to continue your species.

"That sounds intelligent to me. Are you sure we are not the demons your priest claims we are?"

King forced himself to think it through. Though he'd endured many deaths in his time, and survived, somehow he knew that unless he figured out exactly what was happening to him now, at this moment, the Sluagh parasites would rework his DNA to the point where Jack Sigler would no longer exist. Even if his body would live on, King's mind was being rewritten. Changed somehow. A fate worse than death.

"Stop struggling, Jack. It is useless. We have you." Whatever had stabbed him in the base of the neck shifted, sending a new wave of agony through his body. *"You have already failed. Like you failed your friends. Like you failed your team."* She paused. *"Like you failed Sara and Fiona."*

King gritted his teeth against the pain in his neck, then narrowed his eyes at the feminine creature embracing him. *Guilt again. What is it with you trying to make me feel so guilty?*

"Guilt!"

"We love it!"

"It is so, so tasty!"

"We feed. We feast."

"We..."

"...eat it up!"

For a while now, since the larvae had poured out from his neck, the manic multi-voices had ceased. Now, it appeared, they had returned, and King pondered their response to his question.

But guilt is an abstract. You can't feed on an abstract...an emotion.

"We can, if your priest is right." It was the female voice again. *"We can, if we are demons. Emotion, after all, is a product of the spirit."*

Another shift in his spine. A surge of electricity shot through every nerve in his body. He took a breath. Then another, steadying himself once the pain subsided.

It's also a product of chemistry. He thought he could detect the slightest trace of a smile playing up on the side of his face, but he couldn't be sure. A research project he'd read about before being transported nearly three thousand years in the past sprang into his mind.

Cytokines.

The creatures had no response to this, but he could sense their discomfort at the sudden realization. It felt to King as if uttering the word 'Cytokines' had brought a sudden hush on a stadium full of crazed football fans wondering if a referee's flag was going to ruin the game for them.

Cytokines were proteins in the body that affect the autoimmune system. Powerfully negative emotions like guilt and shame play havoc with it, making it more difficult for the body to deal with.

Now, he knew for a fact that he was smiling. He finally understood...at least partly, what the Sluagh were doing. They sought out individuals with high levels of guilt—or rather, disproportionate levels of cytokines—knowing full well their body would have a much more difficult time fighting them off. Even a body with an almost omnipotent immune system like King's still suffered from the chemical effects of guilt.

King hadn't understood all of it when he first read the article. But he'd discussed what he'd read with his fiancée, Sara, a disease detective for the CDC, who'd tried to explain all the intricacies of the research. He'd retained enough to understand that guilt most definitely affected the human body on a physiological level. He understood the horrible way it ravaged a person's immune system. And when you're dealing with a parasitical species, an autoimmune deficiency is as good as an open door and a welcome mat.

"Knowing this will not save you, human."

All pretense of flirtation was gone now. She addressed King as the Sluagh truly saw him—mere meat to absorb, transform and wear like a mobilized suit of undying tissue.

"Your offspring now has your genetic code. They are already re-writing themselves in your image," she said.

Without warning, a flash of silver streaked in front of King's face. A blade, slicing through the female thing's shoulders, forced the creature to release its grip on him. King staggered back, still reeling from the searing pain in his neck, and he looked back to where he'd seen Sara's face. She was no longer there. In her place, was a large sheet of bioluminescent tissue that was vaguely human-shaped.

Anglerfish, remember?

The lovely creature that had been holding him had been little more than an illusion created by the parasites converting his genetic code—making him see and hear whatever they (or she, he wasn't entirely sure how it worked) wanted.

"Are you injured?" Skilurus asked, looking up at him. His sword, tainted with black, decomposing blood, was clutched in his hand. "You were not listening to me. You acted as if you were in pain, and then that...that *thing* grabbed you."

King nodded. "How long was I..." He nodded toward the anglerfish.

"Only a moment. It grabbed you, and then I struck."

It had seemed like hours had passed since walking into the lure's loving arms.

Once again, the creatures' ability to warp reality was both unnerving and impressive. But he had little time to reflect on it. The behemoth creature's mouth snapped shut, slurping in the remainder of his 'offspring', then it shifted its mighty weight to glare at them with baleful eyes.

The two stepped back.

A quick glance over his shoulder confirmed the archer was still hunkered under the doorframe.

"Skil, I'm going to ask you to do something you're not going to like," King said, turning his gaze back to the giant tentacled beast.

"What is your request?"

The creature's bulk twisted again. Its hundreds of tentacles swaying high above them, as if they were giant snakes ready to strike.

"Run."

16

Ursus grabbed hold of Skilurus's wrist and wheeled him around before racing toward the door. The young man chased after his mentor, just as a maelstrom of serpentine arms dropped from the rafters and lunged for them. Midway to the door, Ursus bent down, scooped up his discarded sword and hacked several of the tooth-filled limbs away with masterful precision.

Skilurus didn't like fleeing from the monster behind them, but he understood Ursus's reasoning. The creature was too big. Too powerful for the two of them to defeat at the moment. But there was something else...something that bothered his friend more than the beast's size. Something had happened to him while in its grip. Skilurus had seen the multitude of Sluagh worms pouring from Ursus's neck just before he'd severed the creature's hold on him. He'd seen the near-tidal wave of wriggling bodies inch their way inside the larger creature.

It'd been a ghastly sight. But Skilurus had noticed the color from Ursus's face drain as he'd seen them disappear inside the beast. Ursus rarely showed fear, but he'd been terrified at that moment. Maybe 'terrified' was too harsh a word though. Perhaps 'worried' was more appropriate. But one thing was clear—whatever had happened had clearly affected Ursus, and that was enough to chill Skilurus's core.

More tentacles lashed out at the pair in the twenty-yard sprint to the door, but a few skillful sweeps of their swords kept the appendages at bay. The three of them ran at full speed through the door and down the winding hallway that led to the temple's exit.

The monster howled with rage as its prey escaped. Skilurus thanked the gods that the door was much too small for the creature to easily leave the sanctum sanctorum. Barring any other Sluagh lurking about the Roman outpost, the trio would be outside the city's walls in a matter of minutes, and free to formulate a better plan of attack against the monstrosity they'd just fled.

But when Skilurus entered Isca Silurum's courtyard, he was greeted by a sight he'd least expected to see—Polycarp, pinned down by a hunched-over nude figure, pounding at him with hammer-like fists. Young Clarese, tears streaking her face, stood wringing her hands by the tunnel they'd used to enter the outpost. Too small to fight, all she could do was weep and watch the violent attack unfold before her.

Before Skilurus fully comprehended the scene, Ursus drew his sword and lunged. The figure, sensing the attack, spun around. It grabbed Ursus by the wrist of his sword arm and hurled him with a strength far beyond any normal man.

Their female companion struck next, acting with the same skill and speed as Ursus, but she was just as easily defeated. The man spun to the side, avoiding the woman's strike, and shoved her hard. She tumbled forward, attempting to slow herself, but fell hard to the ground and laid still.

As King flew through the air, his eyes latched on to his attacker's and he recognized the man.

Longinus!

He'd finally awakened. Apparently, he had been healed of his injuries. And now, he was stronger than any man King had faced before. *With strength like that, it's a wonder the Padre is still alive at all.*

King tumbled end-over-end before striking the fortress's wall with the small of his back. A crackle of splintered bone echoed back and forth though the courtyard, as he plummeted to the ground.

"No!" King heard Skilurus shout. He couldn't move his head, but from his peripheral vision, he could make out the sinewy frame of the Neuri youth charging on all fours toward Longinus. There was a fierce growl and the wet sound of flesh and tissue being ripped open. King tried to turn his head for a better look, but his spine had been fractured. He couldn't move his right thumb, much less his head.

"Skil, stop!" he shouted. "You can't beat him!"

Skilurus ignored his pleas. Instead, King saw a blur of motion leaping over the ex-centurion. Snarls and whipping trails of saliva flew through the air with each new attack. From King's vantage point, lying broken on his left side with both his arms stretched in a contorted angle, he could pretty much only see the combatants' feet and legs—dashing here and there—in mortal combat. He wasn't sure whether the growls and snarls were coming from the boy or from Longinus, but he knew beyond doubt that, despite Skilurus's inherited abilities, he was no match for the strength of the mad centurion—especially without his cloak.

Come on! King chastised himself. *Heal, damn it!*

With a sudden snap and a searing jolt of pain, he felt one of his vertebrae pop back into place. He was still paralyzed, but his body was mending itself. Just a little slower than he would have liked.

The cytokines. The guilt fostered by the Sluagh had increased the cytokine cells within his body, dampening his ability to heal. *Too long*, he thought. *It's taking too long.*

With renewed concern, King strained to turn his eyes up for a better view of the fight. A surge of dread swelled in his throat. The boy was holding his own. Or at least, doing the best he could, under the circumstances. And that was what frightened King so much. It shouldn't be possible, but with each swing of the deranged man's powerful arms, Skilurus lunged away, scurried around his attacker on all-fours and tore at Longinus's hamstrings with—*Am I seeing this right?*—elongated canine teeth.

The move was a classic strategy employed by wolves. Decimate their prey's hamstrings, and they would become helpless. But without his ancestral cloak, Skilurus's wolf-like tendencies should have been relegated to something more akin to psychological lycanthropy. Sure, he might act like a wolf, but he shouldn't be able to attain any of the physical characteristics without the cloak of the Neuri people. Even with the cloak, the Neuri weren't actually werewolves. They didn't physically transform into wolves so much as tap into latent primal ferocities akin to canines and other apex predators. But if King was seeing this correctly, something was happening to the boy that was unprecedented...and that unnerved him. He would have to keep a closer eye on Skilurus in the future—if they survived this encounter with Longinus.

A squeal of pain rattled King from his dark thoughts. He returned his attention back to the two combatants to see Skilurus down on the ground; Longinus's filthy, calloused foot was pressed against the young man's skull. Both men were snarling, but the former centurion had finally gained the upper hand. With enough pressure, Skilurus's head would be crushed under the other's formidable, unearthly strength.

17

Longinus stared down at the kid, and his face twisted. His bloodshot eyes narrowed with rage. A string of saliva oozed between clenched teeth. King could sense Skilurus's imminent doom. The crazed man was about to lean forward. Was about to place all his weight down on the boy's head, crushing it like a rotten pumpkin.

He had to do something. But his spine was still busy mending itself. His arms and legs hung limp, unwilling to heed his mental cries to action.

"Longinus, don't!" he shouted. The wild man's head whipped around to glare at him. "You don't want to do this. It's the Sluagh!" King paused, then glanced at Polycarp, who still laid unmoving on the ground a few feet away. "I know. I know what it's like. I know the madness they bring, but you can fight them. We can help you!"

Longinus looked down at Skilurus, then over at the bishop, before alternating his gaze between them, as if in a haze of confusion.

"Let us help you," King continued. His voice nearly cracked as another vertebra popped painfully back into place. "I know you've been fighting them for a hundred years. That fact alone shows just how strong...how courageous a man you really are. Help us to fight them. Help us to send them back to hell, where they belong."

The ex-centurion stood there, staring back at King. His mouth was open, as if about to speak. Something glistened just below both of his eyes. Something crimson and wet. King strained for a better look and realized that the man was bleeding from his eyes. Bloody tears streaked his face. His bloodshot eyes were now completely red, almost obscuring even his irises and pupils. And he shook his head, as if in agony.

"J...just kill me," he hissed between clenched teeth. "They...they will not let me die, but maybe..." His foot against Skilurus's head began to shift back and forth as if preparing to press down. Longinus extended a finger at King, as if unaware of the danger the boy was in. *"...maybe you could kill me. Y...you are different. They fear...fear you."*

"Do not listen to him." For the first time since Skilurus had cut the anglerfish's lure away from King's neck, the female voice had returned.

"No, he lies! He always lies!"

"Lies. Lies. Lies. Lies."

"What have we to fear from you?"

"Maybe you are just as delusional as he?"

"Maybe, you are just..."

"...going mad? Could it be?"

"The immortal Jack Sigler finally losing his mind?"

"Maybe you have been insane all this time?"

"Maybe you are not even immortal?"

King struggled to ignore the voices, but they were too loud now. Impossible to shut out. And as another part of his spine snapped back into place—the pain nearly unbearable—the voices continued to taunt. To nourish old doubts he'd entertained more times than he could count since being stranded in history.

"What if you actually did not go back in time after all..."

"...and you are sitting quietly in a padded cell in a VA Hospital?"

"...That would be funny."

"Shut up," he growled, and then screamed. "Shut up!"

Longinus jumped at King's sudden outburst.

Why am I not healing? My spine should have healed by now. It was his own thought. Not one planted by the invaders within him. It was a good thought. Worth focusing on. Why was his spine not healing faster?

The cytokines, he told himself again. *No, that's just the result. The root cause is...guilt. But of what?*

King stared out toward Skilurus, still struggling to wriggle out from under Longinus's foot. The madman, still shaken by King's outburst, was still staring at him. King still had his attention.

"You see? I'm struggling against them, too. I know what you're going through. You really *can* fight them."

But whatever calm he'd managed to eek from Longinus's psyche was already evaporating. The rapport he'd started to build was visibly crumbling into dust. Longinus's face had resumed its vengeful countenance, and he turned his enraged gaze once more down at Skilurus's helpless form.

"Don't." The single word cut through King's throat like sandpaper. He knew it was useless. Knew there was nothing he could do. Once again, he'd failed to save the life of one of his friends. Once again, he'd failed to protect someone he cared about. Thousands of years on this Earth, and he had never learned his lesson. He was damned, and anyone who traveled with him would always die.

"Yes. Yes."

"Feed us…"

"…with your delectable guilt."

King ignored the voices. All he could do was lie there and watch as the monster who was once Roman Centurion Longinus popped his friend's skull like a grape.

But that was not what happened.

Instead, a tiny sandaled foot stepped toward the madman. King's eyes lifted to see the frail figure of the girl as she approached Longinus.

"Clarese, stop," King growled.

The girl did as she was told and looked back at him. The stains of dry tears streaked her ruddy cheeks. Then she smiled at him. It was the first time she'd so much as acknowledged his existence. The smile itself was as sincere and as comforting as an angel's kiss, and he knew at that moment, he would cherish it for the rest of his immortal life. Then, she returned her gaze toward Longinus.

"You do not have to do this." Her tinkling voice was crisp and cheerful. Innocent and dangerously naïve. Yet her words captivated their intended target. Longinus looked down at her with an expression that King could only describe as wonder. Or was it fear? "You do not have to listen to them." Clarese looked back at King. "Neither do you. You are both forgiven. No need for guilt. No need to endure. You have both been forgiven. Accept it, and do great things."

King felt calm wash over him. The voices inside his mind hushed just before another vertebra popped back into place. Then another. And another. Though the pain was excruciating, King could feel each of the fractured bones in his back repairing themselves almost instantly. Within seconds of the young girl's words, he could feel his own body beneath him once more. Feel the nerves fire to life within his limbs. The fingers of his right hand jerked into motion. His toes wiggled. His shoulders shifted.

He shifted his weight, rolling onto his knees and pushed up with his arms. He could finally move. Almost stand. He had no idea what had happened when the girl had spoken, but he wasn't about to look a gift horse in the mouth. The moment he was able, he'd forge his attack. He would disregard the Padre's wishes and kill Longinus swiftly and without remorse. It was the only way to be sure that this wouldn't happen again.

Clarese, however, no longer seemed concerned over the danger in front of her. She stepped closer to Longinus, extending a hand toward him—an innocent child offering a hand of friendship to a monster.

Longinus blinked at her. His head cocked to one side, confused.

The little girl took one more step closer. She was now within inches of Skilurus, and she crouched down with a bright smile, and stroked the Scythian boy's hair from his eyes.

As King struggled to stand, he watched in amazement as Longinus slowly eased pressure off Skilurus's head, and backed away. Two steps backward, the man put both hands on his hips, and sagged, taking deep mournful breaths, as if an enormous weight had been lifted from his shoulders.

"Thank you," he whispered.

The girl, still beaming, wiped a single stray tear from her eyes, and nodded silently at Longinus. She then turned back to Skilurus, reached a hand out to him, and guided him to his feet. Though bruised and bleeding from numerous scrapes across his neck and arms, he wasn't severely injured. He dusted himself off as he crouched down and took Clarese in his arms.

"I agree," the boy said. "Thank you." He looked past her shoulders at Longinus, and scowled. "This is not over. You and I will have words again, monster."

If Longinus heard the threat, he paid no attention to it. Instead, he cautiously moved over to Polycarp, who was just now beginning to regain consciousness. "I...I am truly sorry," he said, holding his hand out to the priest. Polycarp, to his credit, accepted it without reservation and allowed himself to be hauled to his unsteady feet.

The Bishop of Smyrna shook his head. "No need to apologize, my boy," he said. "A tormented soul needs sympathy and care, not ire and suspicion." He shot King a quick glare of rebuke.

"No, seriously. I'm fine," King said, now standing to his full height. His sword was gripped in his hand. "Thanks for asking."

"As am I," the huntress said, rolling over, face and body covered in mud. She rubbed her head and sat up. Polycarp didn't even glance in her direction.

"You are hardly fine, Ursus," Polycarp replied, not registering the sarcasm in King's comment. He allowed Longinus to slip his arm around his shoulder for support, and lead him over to a shattered pillar that had overturned a few feet away. "I sense the evil within you now."

Longinus nodded. "They are indeed. Your friend is becoming like me, and I am afraid we are both doomed."

King grunted as he limped over to Skilurus. "You okay?"

The boy nodded, his skin still clammy. But he narrowed his eyes and glared at the Roman. "Just my pride, sir. Just my pride."

"Do not change the subject, Ursus!" Polycarp barked behind them. "This is serious, and we need to address the issue now. If you have become host to the Sluagh—

you, of all people—we are in greater danger than ever before. It is not something we can afford to shrug away."

King turned to the bishop. "It's too late. They've already incorporated my DNA into their larvae."

The bishop, Skilurus and Longinus stared back at him, obviously confused.

"My... What makes me...different," he said. "The secret to my..." He glanced around conspiratorially, then specifically at Polycarp, the only one of his companions who seemed to know his secret. "...my longevity. My ability to heal."

"Merciful Savior," the priest gasped.

"And right now, there's a five-ton tentacled slug down in that sanctuary..." King pointed toward the Temple of Augustus, "...trying to figure out how to get out and come after us. So yeah, we've got bigger problems at the moment."

Polycarp glanced over at the temple.

"In there? Now, you say?"

King nodded. "It's trapped inside. For now."

"It is far too large to squeeze through those doors," Skilurus added. "There is no way out."

"You think not, child?" the bishop asked. "Then how, exactly, did it get *in?*"

"It burrowed up from the..." Skilurus stopped, then looked down at the dirt. "Um, from the ground."

Polycarp nodded and glanced over at King. "It is gone. I cannot sense its presence anymore. The only evil in this place resides—" He pointed at King and Longinus, "—in the two of you."

King stepped toward the priest. "Then we track it. Figure out where it's going—just like we did to find this place—and we kill it. Permanently."

"How do we do that?" Polycarp asked. "The Sluagh were nearly invincible before. Now? With your strange condition under their control, I see no path to victory."

18

The campfire popped as King gazed into the dancing flames, pondering the group's next move. It was now into the early morning hours of the next day, and the camp slept peacefully in a well-concealed spot in the southwest quadrant of Isca Silurum. Skilurus was curled in a mound of straw, just yards away from King, where he'd battled a fever all night, after Clarese had bandaged his wounds. Polycarp sat motionless on his knees facing the western wall—deep prayer turned quickly into a much deeper slumber. Clarese, and her huntress-guardian from Geatland, Rhona, were cuddled together on the other side of the fire. Rhona's muscular, tattooed arm rested protectively over the child.

And then there was Longinus. As far as King knew, he was the only other person fully alert at the moment—though he pretended to sleep as well. But no matter how relaxed he seemed, King knew it was all a lie. No one who endured the presence of the Sluagh within them could possibly attain sleep as blissful as the former centurion was trying to project. So, King decided to make the most of the situation.

"I know you're awake," King said. "We should talk."

A few seconds passed, then Longinus sighed and sat up from his bed of fir boughs. "And what should we discuss?"

His voice sounded even. More coherent than King had heard since meeting the crazed man. He wasn't sure if that unsettled him more than anything else he'd encountered.

"We need a plan. A way to kill the Sluagh."

Longinus shook his head. "There is no way to kill them. Especially now. I have heard what they have been saying. Heard their whispers about their power since entering you. They were nearly omnipotent before you came along. Now, they are like the gods."

King growled. "I've met *gods* before. The Sluagh are nothing but worms." A cacophony of curses blared in his mind at his words, but he ignored them. "And you haven't 'heard' anything. They're not speaking to you. Or me. Not really."

"I can hear them even now. As plain as day."

King didn't know how to respond to that. Part of him still wanted to believe that the voices were simply his subconscious trying to make sense of the changes being wrought by the squirmy invaders. But he also couldn't deny their singular, almost coordinated, voice. It was like a hive mind. How else could the worms in Longinus know about King's abilities?

Longinus chuckled. "Your speech patterns are very peculiar, Centurion."

"So I've been told."

There was a lull as Longinus gazed into the campfire for several moments. "I have met only one other person who spoke as you do," he said, picking up a stick from his bedding, and poking it into the fire to watch the tree sap pop. "It was one of *his* disciples, actually. Thomas, was his name. Such peculiar speech patterns."

His voice trailed off, and his eyes glazed over with the unmistakable haze of remembrance.

"Okay," King said, not exactly sure how to respond to the comment, but knowing he needed to get back on topic. "Point is, these worms—intelligent or not—are nothing more than some type of parasite. They can be killed."

"Even with your...DNA?"

King shrugged. "Despite what some people think, I'm not immortal. I'm sure it's possible for me to be killed, though I haven't quite figured out what can do it. But nothing on this world is completely impervious to harm. I've been a soldier long enough to know that for sure. Get a big enough gun, and you can kill it."

"A gun?"

"Never mind. We just need to find the right kind of weapon."

"First, you have to track the thing down." The feminine voice's sudden intrusion into the conversation startled both King and Longinus. They wheeled around to see Rhona crouched down on the outskirts of the campfire's light. King, who had lived and fought wars for nearly a thousand years now, was impressed. He'd not so much as heard her get up from her spot next to Clarese. Though having heard her tale, he couldn't say he was surprised.

She'd told them her story while they'd been setting up camp. She'd come from a village to the north, in Geatland. A band of warriors—precursors to the Vikings from what King could tell—had sacked and killed all able-bodied men there. She and a handful of maidens had been enslaved by their attackers. Like most women in her village, she'd learned to fight, hunt and survive almost from birth. And she'd done all three remarkably well during her time in bondage. Eventually, she'd managed to escape, though she refused to elaborate, and she'd made her way south to the British islands. Seven years ago, she'd been wandering the Welsh plains, when she was waylaid by Roman soldiers, and left for dead on the side of the road. A hunter from Celwyn found her, and brought her back to the village, where she was mended. She'd made it her home ever since, eventually becoming Clarese's guardian, when the girl's parents died after a harsh winter freeze.

"Not sure tracking it will be as easy as it was before," King said. After setting up camp, he, Skilurus and Rhona had returned to Augustus's sanctuary to investigate the tentacled behemoth, but it was gone. The thing had burrowed its way underground, and disappeared without a trace. "We're going to have to outthink it. Figure out where it's heading and meet it there."

"Even if we manage to do that, it still leaves the question of the...um, *gun*, as you put it," Longinus added. "How do we kill something that is almost immortal? How does one kill something made of magic?"

King shook his head. "That's what I've been trying to tell you. These things aren't magic. They're flesh and..." He paused. Something was tickling the back of his mind, but he couldn't quite put his finger on it. "...blood."

Blood.

Why is that sparking a trigger for me?

"You cannot defeat us. No mortal weapon can." It was the female voice again. He'd not heard a peep from her since Clarese silenced the Sluagh earlier that day. He'd hoped they were somehow gone for good, but he should have known better.

"No one can..."

"Defeat us!"

"Not now!"

"Not ever!"

"And soon, we will spread our wings..."

"...and fly..."

"...and hunt..."

"...and kill."

King glanced over at Longinus, who was staring into the fire. They were speaking to him as well, and King could only guess what they were saying. Cautiously, he gripped the hilt of his sword, in case the former centurion was sent into another murderous rage.

"...never find the spear..."

Find the what? He'd been tuning out the Sluagh voices, focusing on Longinus's strange countenance, and he had missed part of the creatures' diatribe. *Never find the what?*

But there was nothing but silence now. It was as if the entire collective residing within him had suddenly gasped, and covered their mouths. As if they'd let something slip they hadn't intended to.

"Find the what?" he said aloud this time.

"What?" Rhona asked. "Beyof, are you feeling well?" *Beyof.* The name she called him. The closest equivalent to 'Ursus' or 'Bear' in her native tongue.

King nodded. "Sorry. The Sluagh were just speaking to me again. Said something that caught my interest, then they stopped."

"The spear." It was Longinus. His voice sounded distant. A thousand miles away. "They are afraid we will find the spear."

"What spear?" Rhona asked.

But Longinus didn't answer. Instead, he continued to stare blindly into the campfire. King watched the man for several long moments, contemplating the demons battling it out within the man's mind. King was about to press the man for answers, when he spoke.

"It was me," he said. "I did it."

"Did..." Rhona said.

"Killed him. Though I knew him to be innocent, I took my spear and pierced his side." Longinus clenched his eyes shut. "He cried in pain, but not for himself." He looked up at King. "He cried out for me."

"Killed *who*?" Rhona asked.

The story's details tickled King's ancient memory, and then, all at once, he understood. He remembered the historical context of Longinus's name.

Longinus pursed his lips, sneering in disgust, and then said, "The Christ."

A heavy silence fell over the group. While Polycarp was the only true believer among them, they all understood the effect of that man's death. None more than King, who had lived in a time when billions believed.

"It is *his* blood they are afraid of," Longinus said.

"Blood?" Rhona cocked her head.

King's eyes widened as Longinus's legend returned to the forefront of his memory. He glanced down at Longinus. "Your spear. The Spear of Destiny."

"Spear of what?" The centurion's face twisted in confusion.

"It's what your spear—the spear that pierced the side of Christ—will become known as," King explained. "Legends throughout the centuries say it possesses supernatural properties. No one knows for sure, because no one knows where it's hidden. But scores of people have searched for it— will search for it."

He heard mumbling from around the camp, as the conversation began to awaken the others, but he continued. "If the Sluagh are afraid of the spear, perhaps it can kill them. They're DNA thieves. Christ's blood, and therefore, his DNA, is on the spear's tip. Maybe something about it is poisonous to them. Or maybe these creatures are supernatural, after all. I don't know. But I know one thing..."

Longinus stood from his seat as well, and for the first time since meeting him, King thought he looked hopeful. "They are afraid of it."

"What is happening?" Polycarp waddled up to the campfire, following by Skilurus, who was wrapping his cloak around him to ward off the chill morning air. "What excites you so?"

"Beyof believes he has found the answer to stopping the demons," Rhona said, glancing back to assure herself that Clarese was still sleeping, despite the commotion.

The priest turned his stern eyes to King. "Do tell."

But King ignored the question. "Your staff, Longinus. Where is it? What did you do with it?"

"I...I..." The former centurion looked so pale in the warm fire's light. Gaunt. His face pulled so tightly across his head, he appeared almost skeletal. His eyes, sunken behind dark brows, closed in obvious shame. "I cannot remember."

19

"What do you mean, you can't remember?" King asked, incredulous. "How could you forget something like that?"

King wanted to scream at the man, but Longinus had no way of knowing that the spear would have any lasting importance. For all he knew, he'd simply tossed the spear during his century-long travels. It could be anywhere in the world. And it was understandable that the spear—the source of Longinus's ultimate shame—would have worn away at him like a millstone around his neck. Discarding the weapon would have been something anyone might have done if circumstances were reversed.

King couldn't even be certain the spear would do anything at all to the Sluagh. For all he knew, it was nothing more than a stick with a blade attached to the end. A normal mortal weapon, undeservedly steeped in legend. Or worse, the Sluagh's verbal slip might be a trap. What if they secretly wanted King to focus on the Spear of Destiny? What if they wanted him to find it?

"I am sorry," Longinus said, his voice so weak it was barely audible.

"Excuse me, Master Ursus," Skilurus said, still holding his blanket around his body. "But what do we hope this spear can do? Why do you think it is the key to stopping these demons?"

King started to answer, then stopped. He wasn't sure. It was more a hunch than anything else. A gnawing at the back of his mind. It was as if the Sluagh influence on his thoughts was somehow translating their own apprehensions into something he could understand. An open door, after all, swings both ways. If they can hear his thoughts…if they could somehow implant ideas into his mind…then why couldn't he do something similar to them?

"I can't explain it," King finally replied. "But right now, it's the only hope we have."

Skilurus nodded his acceptance of the explanation. He was so loyal, it didn't take much to convince him of anything. It was a trait of which King was growing fond. Loyalty like he'd experienced in his first life was hard to come by. He looked around at the group, then stopped on Longinus. "So where do we start?"

The former centurion shrugged, his thumb and forefinger rubbing at the bridge of his nose, as he sat down on his stump in frustration. "I do not...I do not know."

Polycarp frowned, then sat down beside him, putting an arm around the man's shoulder. "It is all right, my son. It will come to you in time."

Longinus shook his head. "No, you do not understand. You cannot." His voice was rising, but he seemed to be in control. "That spear represents everything I loathe. It is the embodiment of my fall. My curse. It was that spear—and what I did with it—that drew the Sluagh to me. Allowed them to haunt my soul. Ravage my mind. Torment my every waking moment and even those brief moments of slumber. I pierced the side of Jesus of Nazareth. An innocent man. More than innocent." He looked up into the sky and sighed.

No one said anything for several moments, then Polycarp cleared his throat. "If Jesus was truly who He claimed, He was not murdered by you or any other single person. He was a divine sacrifice for all mankind." The priest smiled. "Including you, Longinus. Especially you. Do not let that sacrifice be for naught. Release your heavy heart from the shackles of that horrific spear. *Remember.*"

Longinus stared blankly into the fire, rocking back and forth as he pondered the priest's words. King stepped forward, about to speak, but Polycarp silenced him with an upheld hand and a shake of his head.

"There is no redemption for me," Longinus said. "No forgiveness. I am a Son of Cain. Doomed."

Obviously frustrated, the priest squeezed the man's shoulder, and sighed. The rest of the group could only stare, unable to offer anything that might break Longinus from his spell of...

"Guilt," King said, his hand whipping down to the sword at his belt. "Padre, he's experiencing guilt. He's falling under their influence ag..."

But it was too late.

With a roar, the centurion threw the bishop to the side, and lunged headlong at King's midsection before King could draw his blade. The two men crashed backward onto the ground, rolling through the campfire's biting flames, and into the darkness beyond.

"I will kill you," Longinus growled in King's ear, as his vice-like grip struggled to squeeze the life from King's throat. "I will kill you before you find it in the Great Stones."

The crazed man's words were cut short by a right hook from King. It slammed Longinus to the side. Taking advantage of the moment, King scrambled to his feet, then dove on top of the man, wrapping his right leg in between Longinus's legs, and pinning both his arms down.

"Stones?" King shouted. "What stones? What are you talking about?"

Foam and sputum frothed from Longinus's mouth as he growled at King. Dozens of ulcers suddenly erupted over the surface of his body, sprouting hundreds of tiny maggots wriggling their way out from the openings. The pain must have been excruciating, but it only seemed to add to Longinus's strength, which was nothing short of supernatural. It was taking all of King's skill to keep the man restrained.

"Rope!" he shouted. "Someone get rope!"

Before anyone could react, Longinus's hands slipped free, and reached for King's sword. In one swift motion, he pulled the blade from its scabbard, and thrust it deep into King's gut. The familiar burn of ice and fire ripped through King's insides, as the sword slipped through his armor and deep into his bowels. Then, the madman shoved him to the side and bolted away into the darkness. He slipped down into the tunnel that led out of the Roman outpost, and disappeared.

20

King awoke to Clarese's concerned face hovering over his. He hadn't died, that much he knew. But if his healing abilities hadn't returned after his encounter with the Sluagh in Augustus's Temple, he certainly might have.

"Hi," he said to the little girl, wincing as he shifted his weight against the wound.

Clarese smiled and blinked enormous wide eyes at him.

"I was going to heal you," she said. "But you did not need a healer."

King glanced around the camp. He was alone with the girl. "Yeah, I heal kind of fast on my own."

"Is it because of what the big man did to you?"

It was King's turn to blink now. "Big man?"

"You know...the big man with the beard. You call him Alexander."

"How did you know about..."

"Ursus!" Skilurus's shout interrupted his question. "You are awake!"

King wanted to return to Clarese's comments about Alexander, but it would have to wait. There were more pressing matters to address at the moment. He sat up, holding his hand to his side to ease the pain, and nodded.

"Longinus?"

Skilurus's face grew dark, but he no longer appeared ill. "No sign of him. Even Rhona could find no tracks for us to follow. It is as though he sprouted wings and flew away."

Damn it! We had him. We had him, and we let him get away.

"Where're the Padre and Rhona now?" King asked.

"On their way back." Skilurus paused, looking over at Clarese. "They are discussing the girl."

"I have a name, you know." Clarese stuck her tongue out at Skilurus, then smiled. For the first time, King noticed one of her front teeth was missing.

King wondered why the bishop was asking about the girl. She was certainly an unknown variable. Odd, in a cute sort of way. But also, very unsettling. First of all, he'd never heard of a healer or a Druid priestess so young before. Then, there was her uncanny ability to quiet the Sluagh with the sound of her voice. Was it her innocence? Her youthful imperviousness to guilt that garnered such power in her? King decided it was worth further investigation when they had more time. At the moment, the priority was in discovering the location of Longinus's spear.

The sound of Polycarp huffing and groaning as he clambered up the tunnel entrance into the courtyard wrenched King away from his thoughts. He turned to watch the obese old man crawl out into the open with awkward, unwieldy movements. A second later, Rhona followed, her patience with the old man's pace wearing thin.

"Glad you're back," King said to them as they approached. "We have work to do."

The bishop, still panting from his exertion, glanced up at him with a wary eye. "You might have the accursed ability to recover from the most extreme of exertions, but some of us need a few moments to rest."

"Then take a seat, but keep your ears open." King waited for Polycarp to lower himself onto a nearby stump before proceeding. "With Longinus missing, the stakes are higher. I'm not sure what the Sluagh want with him, but from what we've learned about these creatures, he and I are the only living beings they've ever successfully inhabited. Every other account indicates they can only inhabit dead tissue."

"So, what exactly does that mean?" Skilurus asked.

King shook his head. "No idea. But even though they're still inside me, their influence seems to have dissipated. I think they're pretty much finished with me. So the question is, what do they want with Longinus? What's their plan, and why did they drive him away from us?"

"That seems simple enough," Rhona responded. "Surely, to keep us from learning the location of his spear."

"Possibly," King said, thinking about the stones Longinus had mentioned and whether or not that was him speaking, or the Sluagh. "The worms are keeping possession of him for a reason, and that's something we should be concerned about. No good can come from it, I can promise you that."

"So what do we do? Look for the spear, track down Longinus or go after the Sluagh?" She asked. "Or do we split up and pursue all three?"

King pondered the question. She was making a good point. Whereas before, they only had one goal, now their attentions were being divided, possibly by design. After a moment, he returned his gaze to Rhona. "I don't think we'll need to divert our search at all."

"What do you mean?"

"I mean that Longinus lost control when the Sluagh feared we were getting too close to discovering their Achilles Heel."

"Their what?" Skilurus asked.

"Their weakness. The thing that can destroy them. I believe Longinus, under the Sluagh influence, is heading for the spear now. He's probably going to try to destroy it or hide it somewhere else." He began kicking dirt on the fire, smothering the flames, as the orange-red strip of the rising sun crested over the eastern horizon. "And I think the Sluagh will follow him. As backup. To protect him from us. To ensure the spear is destroyed."

"How can you be sure?" Rhona asked.

King shrugged. "I can't. But it's what I would do if the roles were reversed." He sighed. "I've been going at this all wrong. I believed the Sluagh were nothing but mindless worms. I was wrong. I'm not sure what they are, but I do believe they have a purpose. Some sort of intelligence is driving them, no matter how primitive it might be. These things can think, which means they can strategize. Their best chance at survival is to destroy the one thing that can end their lives."

"Sounds reasonable," Rhona said. "But we still have the issue of tracking. I searched high and low around the outpost's perimeter. Other than a few tracks just outside the walls, I found nothing to follow. It is as if..."

"I heard. Sprouted wings. Or maybe he's taken to the trees. Or more likely, underground...following the burrow left by the giant creature in the sanctuary." King glanced over at Skilurus. "Start breaking down camp and pack the horses. We're heading out." The Neuri set to work without another word, allowing King to continue. "No, I think our best bet isn't to track Longinus. It's to beat him to the spear."

"And how do we do that?" Polycarp asked. Clarese was sitting in his lap, her head resting comfortably on his broad shoulders. "We have no idea where it is."

"Longinus gave us a clue as to its location."

"The 'Great Stones,'" Rhona said. "That could be anything. Anywhere. It might not even be here in Britannia."

"True. But if the weapon was a powerful source of guilt for Longinus, perhaps he carried it until recently. If it was far away, they wouldn't fear it the way they do."

"Even if that is true," Polycarp said, "this is a very big island."

King nodded. "It is. But the Sluagh don't have complete control of Longinus either. We know the spear was hidden. It wasn't destroyed. Perhaps there was a part of Longinus that wanted to keep it safe. Maybe he couldn't bear to be rid of the object of his perceived curse. Maybe he developed an unhealthy dependence on it. Either way, the Sluagh should have destroyed it once they had no more use for it, but they didn't. Or they couldn't. I suspect Longinus wouldn't destroy it for them, so they opted to hide it instead."

Rhona shrugged. "This still does not help us locate it."

"But it does. Let's say you had an attachment to something. Something you couldn't bear to be separated from for the rest of your life. You had to hide it, but you knew you'd want to maybe come back for it one day. What is the one thing you'd ensure when you hid it?"

Rhona and Polycarp sat in silence, considering their answers to the question.

"You would want to know where you hid it," Clarese spoke up. "I know exactly where I hid my doll, when the monsters came to our village the other day. I can take you right there without even thinking about it."

King smiled at her. "Exactly. If you're going to hide something, you're going to want to remember where you put it."

"But Longinus could not remember. He could not tell us," Polycarp said.

"His mind was warped by the Sluagh's influence. You don't know what it's like. Dozens of voices shrieking at you at one time. It's hard to decipher where your thoughts end and theirs begin. But if his words prove true, the location he hinted at came from him, not the Sluagh."

"The Great Stones." Rhona repeated. "But Britannia is covered in stones. Cliffs. Rocky beaches. There are stone monuments everywhere. Where would we even begin to look?"

"Monuments." King said it almost without thinking.

"Like I said, there are stone monuments everywhere on this island."

"But only one that could be called great." King stood. "Stonehenge."

21

They rode as fast as their horses could carry them, with Skilurus riding behind Rhona, who was much better with horses than the youth. The distance from Isca Silurum to Stonehenge was close to seventy miles. The terrain, rich with rolling grasslands, a few rocky inclines scattered here and there and the occasional creek or river, put their journey at about a two and a half days' ride. King wanted to cut that time in half, so he pushed the horses and his companions harder than was humane. There was too much at stake for anything less.

King wasn't sure how fast the Sluagh could travel—whether in its huge anglerfish form or as individual larvae—but he was willing to bet that Longinus had already stolen a horse and was well on his way. So he had no choice but to ride as fast as possible, in hopes of beating the madman to the ancient monument.

They'd already been riding for most of the day, and the sun was dipping over the horizon. Soon, they'd be forced to stop for the night to rest and water their horses. It was time they didn't have to waste, but it had to be done.

"It does not have to be," said the female voice inside his head. *"What has this world ever done for you?"*

"It tore you away..."

"...away from your friends and family!"

"It turned you into a freak of nature..."

"...and has tormented you..."

"...more than we ever could!"

Just shut up. I'm in no mood to deal with you right now.

"And it is just beginning!" The voices, apparently, had decided to ignore his demand.

"How long must you endure this?"

"How many times must you die?"

"How many times must you act?"

"How many times must you..."

"...play the hero for the ungrateful masses?"

I said, be quiet!
"You do not have to, you know."
"Just turn around."
"Just give up."
"Just quit while you are ahead."
"I said, SHUT UP!"

The moment the words exploded from his lips, his companions turned to stare at him, concern painted across their faces. It seemed the Sluagh inside him had decided to change tactics. They'd given up on fostering overwhelming feelings of guilt, and had moved on to destroying his confidence. Or rather, the confidence his team had in him.

They'd instigated his outburst. Refused to relent until he could take it no longer. And now, with the looks of pity and suspicion his friends were giving him, it looked as if the Sluagh's plan could work, if he let it. The worms had chipped away a small piece of the team's confidence in him. In the end, it wouldn't matter, King knew. Polycarp and Skilurus would follow him to the end of the world and back. He couldn't be sure the same was true for Rhona and her young charge, but then, King had protested having Clarese come with them to begin with. If they wanted to back out now, it would be one less person he'd have to worry about dying before his eyes. One more person he might fail.

Easy, Sigler. You're dangerously close to guilt again.

After a few more miles, King brought the riders to a halt. They set up camp near a stream hidden by a stand of fir trees. Once settled, they ate a brief supper, then settled down for a short night. Once again, King took first watch. With his remarkable metabolism, it was rarely necessary for him to sleep. When he did, it was simply to enjoy the slumber. So he rested, his torso raised up on his elbows with his back to the fire, and looked out into the night.

A few minutes passed, when he heard a few short shuffling sounds behind him. He craned his head to see Clarese waddling up to him with large, sad eyes. Without a word, she sat down next to him, put her head across the leather armor covering his abdomen, and sighed.

"Uh, are you..." King wasn't sure what to say. Except for a few brief moments, the girl had said very little to him, and had expressed no real connection with him at all. King liked children. Or at least, he used to. But he'd met far too many who'd died too young. Or worse, grown up to disappoint him in horrific ways. He'd learned long ago that it was unwise to grow too attached to them. "...are you okay?"

She looked up at him, gracing him with a weak smile before placing her small hand in his. "Are you?"

He blinked at her, uncertain how to respond. Fortunately, she took the necessity away.

"They are still talking to you."

King nodded.

"What do they say?"

"All sorts of things. It's not really something you should worry yourself—"

"Bad things, I assume."

He offered another nod, realizing she wasn't going to let it drop.

"Things about your past? Failures? People you left behind?"

This time he didn't nod. He had, instead, decided to listen to where Clarese was taking her questions.

"People like Fiona? Sara?"

King went rigid. His hand pulled away from hers. It was the second time she'd seemed to divine very specific details about his past. "Who...what are you?"

Her smile widened, though it still seemed sad to him. "I am Clarese."

Reluctantly, he returned her smile, though he wasn't sure why. He had to remind himself that the girl was only six years old, though she sometimes acted as though she was sixty.

"You know," she continued, "you remind me a lot of my father. He used to get sad like you. All the time. Sometimes, he would just stare off into the stars for hours on end. Sometimes, I would see him cry, which always made me cry, though I never knew why."

"And your mother? How did she react to your father's tears?"

Clarese gave a curt shrug. "Ma died when I was a baby. I never knew her. Rhona is as close to a mother to me than anything I ever had."

"I'm sorry."

She giggled at that. "That Rhona is like my Ma? That is silly. I love her."

King laughed, too. "No, I'm sorry that you lost your parents. That must have been hard."

She stayed there—her head still resting in his lap—and pondered his statement. After a moment, she shook her head. "I do not think it was nearly as hard as what you have gone through." She looked back up at him. Her face had turned stone serious. "Or what you still have to endure, I think." He started to respond to that, but she cut him off again. "You know, our journey here will not end the way you expect. You will suffer great loss. A loss that you cannot quite explain, which will lead you to be tormented by horrible grief for years to come. And then, after you think you have defeated them, you will still have to face the *Grundling*."

Clarese had said so much in that last moment, King's head practically reeled as he tried to decipher it all. *Our journey won't end the way I expect? Suffer great loss? Tormented by grief?* In the end, the only question he could formulate was, "The *Grundling*?"

She nodded her head solemnly. "That is what *they* call him anyway. The Sluagh, that is. They call him the Grundling. The Sluagh King." She paused, reaching out for King's hand again and clutching it tightly. "He Who Is Birthed from the Ground. The Grundling. The Son of Cain."

"Longinus? You're saying Longinus is the Grundling? The King of the Sluagh?"

She closed her eyes before shaking her head. "No, not poor Longinus. He is a tormented soul, just like you. No, the Son of Cain. The Son of Cain is the Grundling, not Longinus."

King was as confused as ever. The Sluagh had constantly referred to the former centurion as the Son of Cain. Clarese, however, was insisting that he was not. Who was telling the truth? And how could a six year old girl know such things?

He started to question her more, but she shifted her body, curling it into a ball and gripping his hand even tighter. "I am very sleepy now, Beyof," she said, calling him by the name Rhona used. "I want to sleep now. Like I used to when I was smaller...curled up in my Da's lap."

King looked down at her tiny, dirt encrusted hand. So small. So fragile. And so at ease within his own palm. Within seconds, her breathing became deeper. Steadier. Signs that she was already well on her way to unconsciousness. Gently, using his other hand, he brushed the tangled mess of curls away from her face and watched her as she slept. Before long, as he glanced down into that reflection of innocence, he forgot all about monsters and danger and unnerving prophecies, and fell asleep as well.

22

Stonehenge
Salisbury Plain

The remainder of the journey went without incident, and the companions found themselves moving at a slow trot across the Salisbury Plain around three in the afternoon the next day. The megalithic monument—so familiar in King's own time—jutted up in the distance like the decomposing spine of some long dead leviathan, and a collective gasp echoed from the mouths of his friends as they took it all in.

"This is Stonehenge," King said, as their horses pushed toward the ancient monument.

"By the gods," Skilurus said in a reverent tone. "What is it? What is it used for?"

"No one knows for sure." Of course, King had been here once before. A long time ago. In the future. So long ago now that he could barely remember the reason for his visit, or what had transpired when he was there. He knew it had involved a mission of some kind. And monsters made of stone. But beyond that, it was all a bit hazy at the moment. "It's been here a very long time. No one knows who built it or why, but it has captured the imaginations of the greatest minds of almost every generation."

Why do I know that, but can't remember my last visit here?

"Maybe because you failed here," the female voice in his head said with a cackling laugh. *"Just as you will fail here today."*

King ignored the voice and glanced at Clarese, riding in front of Polycarp. She gave him a comforting nod and a smile. *She knows. She knows they're trying to mess with me, even now.* Whoever the little girl was...*whatever* she was...there was something special about her.

As they'd packed up camp to start on the day's journey, King had questioned Polycarp about his conversation with

Rhona regarding the child. He'd been tight-lipped, stating that their discussion had been in the strictest of confidence. The old priest had seemed very sad the moment the girl was brought up, but refused to elaborate.

All King knew was that when he was in her presence, the Sluagh's influence always seemed muted. Contained somehow. And with Clarese's little hands wrapped around his, he'd had the best night of sleep he'd experienced in decades. He also knew that when this was all over, he was going to delve deeper into her mystery.

For now, however, he set aside all other thoughts and focused on the megalithic structure as they crested a small hill. Once everyone had caught up, he motioned for his team to halt. Then he got down from his frothing horse. The others followed suit, and huddled together to discuss the next phase of the plan.

"First things first," King said, as he looked each person in the eye, one by one. "We're in an open field. There's no cover. If Longinus or the Sluagh are there, they'll see us coming."

"We have already seen you. You and your friends are as good as dead."

Ignoring the voice in his head, he continued. "That said, we still need to do reconnaissance—check out the situation. We've no idea what's waiting for us. No idea where the spear is hidden. We're going in blind."

"We will enjoy wearing your skin..."

King looked at Rhona. "You're a hunter. How's your eyesight?"

"I would wager the best of this lot." She paused. "Except, for maybe you."

"We will especially enjoy wearing the brat."

"The brat. Her skin will feel so warm."

"So comfortable."

"So soft."

King ground his teeth. Then, he felt something grab his hand. He looked down to see Clarese staring up at him. The voices fell silent at her touch. He squeezed her hand back, and resumed plotting their strategy. When everyone knew what they were supposed to do, Polycarp gathered them all around him, and he said a prayer on their behalf.

"Now, since Ursus has seen fit to keep me from the fray," the bishop glared at King, "Clarese and I will stay here and keep vigil for the three of you. Go with God, my friends."

Without another word, Rhona, Skilurus and King broke away from their horses, then jogged to the nearest stone—a menhir two hundred yards away from the monument proper. Using the menhir as a blind, Rhona peered around the edge and scanned ahead.

"See anything?"

"I do not need eagle eyes to see they are already here and waiting for us."

Curious, King peered around the other corner of the stone. "Well, shit."

Although there was no sign of Longinus or the giant anglerfish creature, two very large, very brutish looking giants loomed in the center of the ring. The creatures, both nearly twelve feet tall, seemed disproportionate from this distance. Their arms and legs were comprised of limbs that didn't match. Right arm, big and muscular. Left arm, slight and feminine. The left arm of the giant on the right had been torn off at the elbow, and in its place, three whip-like tentacles flailed back and forth in anticipation of the coming fight.

The skin of both creatures was loosely stitched together, revealing muscle, sinew and bone. The left giant's face was incomplete, having no flesh around the jaw except a few strands of tendon that held it in place. Both sported numerous stretched-out faces over their chests, abdomens and even arms. Even more unsettling, the faces still contained eyes that moved back and forth, as if performing sentinel duty.

King pulled back and leaned against the menhir. "I'm betting that those Watchers are standing where we need to be."

"But there are just two of them," Skilurus said. "Surely, the three of us can—"

"It's not the two of them that bothers me," King said. "It's the others we haven't seen yet."

"Then we need to draw them out," Skilurus said.

Before King could protest, the Neuri darted into the open and sprinted toward the monsters.

"Skilurus, stop!"

If he heard King, the boy didn't respond. Instead, he picked up speed, leaned forward and began running on all fours. The watchers reacted without hesitation. With the simultaneous grace of two defensive linemen, they charged Skilurus, swinging their massive fists at him. The boy ducked lower to the ground as the mallet-sized fists swung past his head, then rolled between the right one's legs before skittering to the other side of the stone ring.

The two watchers spun around and were rewarded with three arrows piercing their skulls from behind. King turned to see Rhona lining up her fourth shot just before releasing it and striking another blow.

King ran from his blind to help Skilurus with the giants. When he was within ten feet, he drew his sword, and leapt. He twirled the sword mid-air, landed on the nearest creature's back, and brought the blade down into its spine. It screamed, spinning around to locate its attacker, but King clung out of reach. The creature's flesh reeked of decomposing gasses. Its skin felt rubbery—sponge-like—making it difficult to maintain his hold. Then, as the watcher whirled around a second time, its thin epidermis began to slough away from its neck, sending King spiraling to the ground.

Enraged, the giant stretched its enormous arm behind its back and lunged for the sword still lodged there. But its reach wasn't quite long enough, and it fumbled pathetically in its attempt to ease its pain. A moment later, three more arrow shafts plunged deep into its spine, and the creature stumbled to its knees with a roar.

King nodded his thanks to Rhona, still secure behind the menhir, then leapt to his feet, darted around the watcher and pulled his sword from out of its back. He knew the arrows were only a temporary reprieve. He had only seconds to act. Of course, if his DNA had already been transferred to all of the Sluagh, then this entire endeavor was doomed. It still didn't dissuade him. He gripped the sword's hilt tightly in his hand, spun a full three hundred and sixty degrees and then brought the blade down against the creature's neck with all his strength. He was rewarded by the sickening wet slap of the blade's edge slicing through muscle and tendons. But it didn't slice all the way through, and it was now embedded in the watcher's spinal cord. King reached for the sword's handle again, but before he could grab it, two slender tentacles whipped out from his left, and coiled around his neck, yanking him three feet off the ground.

Surprised by the sudden attack, King's eyes searched for the new attacker and found the second watcher, its third tentacle wrapped around Skilurus's chest, squeezing the life from him. He glanced back at the first giant, who was now beginning to lumber to his feet. He eyed the sword still buried in its neck, just out of reach. Then it stumbled back a step, as it stood.

Like a viper, King's hand whipped out, grabbed the sword's hilt, and yanked the blade away from the watcher's neck. Before either of the monsters could react, he turned the blade on the tentacles around his throat, and cut himself free. Then he rolled away and leapt toward Skilurus, hacking away the tentacle around his chest. The now tentacle-less creature backhanded him away.

The impact sent King through the air, where he was caught by the first watcher. Its one, trunk-like arm curled around King's midsection and began to constrict, shoving his abdomen toward his spine with violent, ear-splitting pops.

"Stop!"

The giant didn't hesitate. But the moment the word was uttered, its crushing arm eased and King found himself breathing again. Curious, he looked in the direction of the voice.

Longinus's grim face glared back at him.

23

Longinus had changed since he ran away from Isca Silurum two days before. His skin was pale. Almost gray. Clumps of his long hair had fallen out. Boils, the size of Skilurus's fists, had popped up all over his body. And dozens of larvae now covered almost every surface of his exposed body.

Instead of the rags he'd been wearing since they last saw him, he was now adorned in his Roman uniform. The bronze chest plate and helmet gleamed in the afternoon sun. His maroon cloak, crusted with dirt and grime, hung in tatters around his shoulders. And in his right hand, he held a long, tarnished spear.

King took it all in, then noticed Rhona lying unconscious—her chest rising and falling with each breath—at his feet. Polycarp stood beside Longinus, the twisted centurion's free hand holding him close. The bishop held Clarese in his arms, but Longinus's spear point hovered inches from her neck.

"Yes! Yes! Skin her!"

"We will wear her like a coat."

"Peel the flesh from her bones!"

"Just to watch her die."

The voices in King's head all started cackling, but there was nothing he could do. He was trapped in a watcher's hulking arm. Skilurus was still on the ground, struggling to regain his breath after having it squeezed from him. For the moment, he was at the mercy of Longinus and the Sluagh. He would simply have to bide his time until an opportunity presented itself...or he managed to create one for himself.

"I am here to make you a proposition, Strange One," Longinus said. The watcher lowered King to the ground, and took a single step back, as the former centurion continued. "The life of your friends for one simple thing in return."

"And that is?"

"Come with me. Allow me to introduce you to my mother."

"And?"

Longinus shrugged. "That is all. I have the spear now, so she has nothing to fear from you." He withdrew the spear's tip from Clarese's neck as a show of good faith. "She wants to see you...with her very own eyes."

Something gray-white was moving along the ground behind Longinus, catching King's attention. He focused on the movement, only to realize it was a mass of Sluagh larvae writhing over the southern hill bank, moving toward them like a tidal wave. There were thousands of them.

"Then what? I doubt 'seeing' me is really all that high on her agenda." He kept his eyes fixed on the approaching river of maggots washing toward Stonehenge, and he tensed.

"My mother's plans are hers alone." Longinus shrugged, then stepped into the stone ring, bent down and picked up King's sword from the ground. He gave it a heft, smiled, then slid it into his belt. "All I know is that I have finally stopped fighting them and have never been more at peace. No more guilt. No more sorrow. You can finally have this peace as well."

"And if I don't accept this peace, you'll kill my friends?"

"I will not enjoy it." He glanced at each of his captives; his eyes lingered a little too long on Rhona. "But I will if necessary, yes."

The front line of the maggot wave reached Longinus and stopped, presumably awaiting orders.

You will still have to face the Grundling. King remembered Clarese's words to him the night before. The Grundling. King of the Sluagh. The Son of Cain. Longinus, but not Longinus. He didn't know what to make of her prophecy.

After a moment, King nodded. "Okay. I'll go with you. But if there's anything left of the real you in there, I want your vow...my friends will remain safe." He thought about his words a moment, then added, "And unchanged."

Longinus smiled, revealing hundreds of tiny squirming maggots where his teeth had once been. "You have my vow. No harm. No change. They are safe, as long as you remain faithful to our deal."

"Ursus, no!" Polycarp shouted, then winced as Longinus tightened his grip around the bishop's arm. But the old man wouldn't relent. "You know as well as I that it is a trap."

Longinus laughed. "It most certainly *is* a trap. But one into which Ursus will gladly walk."

King resisted the urge to growl, and instead, gave one, curt nod of his head. "I will."

"Excellent!" Longinus released his grip around the bishop's arm, and the swarm of larvae rushed past their legs and squirmed their way inside the stone ring. The watcher holding Skilurus down on the ground, carefully scooped him up, allowing the maggots to pass. The wave of larvae swept past King and the watcher behind him. They came to a stop near the sacrificial altar erected at the center of Stonehenge. Then, one by one, the hundreds of thousands of worms began to dig in unison.

"Do you have any idea what this place is, Ursus? What it was originally used for?"

King shook his head as he watched the maggots shovel away at the rocky soil, creating a large tunnel deep beneath the monument. "Some say it was some type of calendar," he said. "A way to map the stars and the sun. The days of the year." He turned back to look at Longinus. Countless worms had pushed through the skin of the centurion's face, and now wriggled their gray-white bodies in precise rhythm with one another. "Others say it has a much less mundane purpose. A mystical purpose. If I remember right, a friend of mine once had a laboratory underneath here. Who knows the true purpose of its builders, really?"

"We know," Longinus said, with a worm-filled smile. "The Sluagh have always known. It is what drew us here. Why we felt compelled to hide the spear here. And why mother has rested here ever since." Longinus gestured to the center of the ring, and King turned and saw that the sea of maggots had disappeared down into the tunnel they had burrowed into the ground. "After you."

King watched as Skilurus's watcher lumbered toward Polycarp, Clarese and Rhona, then laid the boy down next to the huntress.

"Oh, do not worry. My sentries will keep a watchful eye on them. Keep them safe. A promise, after all, is a promise."

King let Longinus's words sink in for a moment. He found it interesting that the more control the Sluagh seemed to gain on the Roman, the more modern his speech patterns became.

He stepped toward the tunnel and stooped down to enter, but after several feet, the ceiling and walls opened wider, and he was able to stand.

"Are you going to tell me what this place really is?" King asked as the two of them walked down the tunnel. He glanced back, but already, his companions were out of view. He wasn't sure whether he'd ever see them alive again, and he was beginning to wrestle with whether he'd made a mistake leaving them alone with those monsters above.

"It was a cairn of sorts. A tomb."

"Seems rather elaborate for a grave. Stonehenge does track the stars. That's not theory. It's fact. It's like mounting a clock on a gravestone. It doesn't make sense."

It was growing darker. The entrance was nearly obscured from view, and the little light still seeping through was growing dimmer with each step.

"It does if there was a time limit for the dead to stay dead," Longinus said. King felt hot breath against his ear, as if the former centurion had whispered conspiratorially in his ear. "It was not humans that were buried here, Ursus. It was giants."

Giants. King remembered legends of Stonehenge's origins. Some said that Merlin had used giants to construct the megalithic structure. But the giants had been here long before Merlin's time.

"They were monsters. Revered by the ancient peoples that built this place," Longinus continued. It was now completely dark, and King felt the Roman take hold of his arm guiding him the rest of the way. "In reality, they were our descendants, who came from..." The man looked toward the ceiling.

King felt the ground level out, and the tunnel began to brighten with a soft yellow-orange glow. He looked around and found himself in a larger, much older tunnel. This one was comprised of thick stone walls, which were spider-webbed with miles and miles of vine-like tentacles emitting some sort of bio-luminescent light. The tentacles, similar in almost every way to those of the Sluagh, squirmed along the walls and ceiling with wet, slurpy movements.

"Mother has been down here ever since, bonding with the corpses of our ancestors. Drawing upon their..." He paused as if trying to find the right word. "DNA, as you call it, to make herself stronger."

King turned three-hundred and sixty degrees within the hallway he now stood in, taking in every detail. Behind the tentacles, carved deep into the stonework, he could see drawings depicting a world filled with gigantic slug-like creatures. Frail-looking humans bowed down to them. Some were depicted as being sacrificed. Some were being consumed by the largest of the monsters. But no matter where he looked, there were no depictions of anything remotely hopeful. Humanity, during this time, had been enslaved.

They stopped at an arch—similar in every detail to the stone arches of the monument above them—that opened up into an enormous chamber. Longinus motioned for King to enter first, still clutching his spear.

King hesitated. "Let me ask you something first."

The Roman nodded his permission.

"The voices in my head. Are they real? Is the female voice your 'mother'? Am I really hearing them?"

Longinus closed his eyes as if in thought, then shrugged. "We do not communicate the same way that you do. In reality, without the use of this human mind inside me, I would not be able to speak to you." He tapped his left temple with his index finger. "But each of our colonies has a parent. It attaches itself to the base of our spine, and begins replicating itself inside us. The more of them there are, the more of your essence—that DNA material you mentioned— they tap into. They siphon it off. Absorb it into themselves, and inject their own essences into you. It is not so much that they speak to you. It is more like the closer you become to being like them, the more you know about them. The more you think like them."

"And you're saying I'm being made into one of them?" King watched as the worms inside Longinus's mouth waggled back and forth. "Like they're doing to you?"

"Normally, they are unable to inhabit and transform a living host. That is why they need dead tissue, though they are capable of killing a living host if need be. However, you and I are different from most other mortals. I..." He touched his spear hand to his chest. "...am cursed. A descendent of Cain. And you...you are something else entirely. We do not know what to make of you. But your essence is beyond our wildest imaginings." Once again, he gestured to the archway. "Now, enough stalling. She will see you."

With nothing more to say, King stepped through the door and quickly reconsidered the wisdom of his actions.

24

The thing inside the chamber was beyond anything King had ever seen before. It was an amorphous blob of human and animal tissue, twenty-five feet around, and covered in eyes, hair, nails and teeth. It had no eye sockets, or mouths—except for those at the tips of its dozens of tentacles still confined within the room. No arms, hands, legs or feet. Like all other Sluagh, this creature's body was bloated with decomposing flesh. Venous streaks of green marbling and pockets of blisters filled with dark, bloody fluid covered its mass.

It swelled and deflated at regular intervals, as if the monster was breathing. With each rise and fall of its form, the blisters popped and spewed their cadaverous liquids all around it.

The thing reeked as well. The entire chamber was filled with the putrid stench of methane, ammonia and stagnant swamp water.

"Behold," Longinus said, stepping into the chamber with him. "Our mother."

"You keep saying 'our'. I'm assuming you mean you and the other Sluagh."

The Roman chuckled at this. "Yes. But I am also referring to you. After all, you are just as much a part of this as I am." King felt Longinus's spear point press into his back. "Now, step closer. Mother wants a word with you."

"I think I'm close enough, thanks," King said, pressing his back against the spear's tip.

"You really have no choice," the female voice inside his head said. Her words almost seemed melodic, like she was singing a lullaby to him.

"No choice."

"No choice."

"You are one of us."

"Embrace who you are!"

"Give in..."

"Give up..."

"Be us."

"You are really starting to make me angry," King said aloud. He wasn't concerned about sounding insane now, since none of his companions were around to hear him.

"You gave your word, Ursus," the Roman said.

"I said I'd come down and see this monstrosity. I never said I'd..."

Longinus struck him with the butt of his spear, driving him to the ground. "Do not insult her!"

The impact sent King to the ground, a foot closer to the blob-like Sluagh. Rubbing the back of his head, King turned and looked at the former centurion. "Longinus, listen to yourself," he said. "This isn't you. You don't want this. You've been fighting these things for a hundred years. Don't give up now."

"He cannot hear you, King. He can only hear me now." Before he could respond, four tentacles shot down, grabbing King by all four limbs, and jerking him up into the air. *"Now, it is time to complete what we began in the Caesar's temple."*

"It's not going to work. I figured out the way you work. Your power is my guilt, and I'm not going to allow you to feed on mine any longer. I'm free of you!"

"Really?" Longinus asked.

The tentacles turned King toward Longinus—toward the door—just as Skilurus and Rhona were shoved into the chamber by another set of tentacles. Then, Polycarp, still clutching Clarese. They were conscious and didn't seem to be injured, but their presence changed everything.

King looked at them, then back at Longinus.

"We had a deal! You said they'd be safe. Unharmed and unchanged."

"The Son of Cain had no authority to deal on my behalf."

King twisted around to look at the giant creature throbbing in the center of the chamber. He pulled at the serpentine bonds holding him several feet above the ground, but couldn't break free.

"I am sorry, Ursus," Longinus said. "This is the only way for you to reach your true state. One by one, they will each die as you watch...as you realize that their deaths are because of you. Because you failed them."

"As you failed your Chess Team."

"As you failed Sara..."

"...and Fiona."

"These four will now die..."

"...and it will be entirely your fault."

The tentacles twisted King around, forcing him to watch as Longinus walked to Skilurus and placed the spear tip against his chest. Skilurus glared back and let out a brave snarl.

"Which one will die first, Ursus?" He raised the spear up to Skilurus's neck, and dragged the tip lightly across his throat. A ribbon of red swelled where the blade had scratched his skin.

"Don't do this, Longinus!" King screamed. "Remember who you are!"

Ignoring him, Longinus stepped to Rhona. "Perhaps this Geatish beauty? You only just met her, after all. Perhaps it would be a mercy to start off with the one you care about the least." The huntress lifted her chin up in defiance. Her lips curled in a sneer. "Then again, 'mercy' will not accomplish what must be done."

Longinus took another step to his right to eye Bishop Polycarp and the little girl he still held in his arms. "Now these two..." He turned around to look at King. His worm-filled grin stretched the contours of his face in an impossible caricature of its former self. "These two are something very special to you, are they not?" Longinus raised a hand, and gently stroked Clarese's cheek with his left hand. "Especially this little one. You have grown quite fond of her."

"Skin her!" cried one of the voices in his head.

"Wear her like a cloak."

"Feed on her and swallow her whole!"

King thrashed against the tentacles holding him aloft.

Longinus held up his free hand, and gave a single, reserved nod. "I will tell you what," he said. "We will let you."

The tentacles lowered King to the ground and released him. He took a single step forward, before he was blocked on all sides by a wall of the mother's wormy appendages.

"Let me what?" he asked, certain he wasn't going to like the answer.

"Choose. Then, kill your choice."

"If you do this," the female inside his head said, *"The others will be released."*

"Without harm," Longinus continued. "Without change." The Roman stepped forward, pulled King's sword from his belt, and appraised it. "This is a fine weapon. Ancient Greek, is it not?"

King didn't respond, prompting Longinus to let out a soft sigh of disapproval. The tentacled cage spread apart, and the former centurion walked up to King, turned the blade around in his hand, and held the hilt out for him to take. "Your weapon is returned. Choose wisely, or they will all die."

25

King looked over at his friends, still entangled in the web of tentacles that held them in place. They'd been silent since entering the chamber, though most of them had been unable to pull their eyes away from the Sluagh mother since seeing her for the first time. Now, each of them were returning his gaze. Each with a stalwart defiance against their captors that made him proud.

"Who will it be, Ursus?" Longinus asked.

"I'm telling you, it doesn't have to be this way," King said, gripping his sword. "You can fight them."

"You keep saying that, as if I have any desire to fight them. Trust me, I do not." Longinus leveled his spear at King. "Now, please. Stop stalling and choose."

King looked down at his sword, then at each of his friends, and finally he returned his gaze to Longinus. He gave a nod of resignation, and sighed. "Fine." He stepped up to Skilurus, and raised his blade up to the young man's chest. To his credit, Skilurus never so much as blinked. He simply stood there, staring back at King. Complete trust etched on his face. "I'm sorry, Skil. For everything. I've never trusted your kind...not since I first encountered them two hundred years ago. They were primal. Fierce. And had no concept of honor."

A single tear stained Skilurus's face as he listened to King. His lips quivered, but he continued to keep his chin up and looked King square in the eyes without interruption.

"It was the chieftain of your tribe who was to blame," King continued. "I know that. But he killed, then ravaged, a companion of mine. Set his body on a spit and feasted on him for days. I've never been able to forgive him, or your people for that...even after all these years."

"What are you doing, King?" the mother asked, a nervous quiver in her ethereal mental voice.

"So, I've taken it out on you. I'll admit it." King lowered his head apologetically. "I've treated you poorly. I've refused to trust you, even though you've been nothing but the most loyal of friends since we met. I destroyed your cloak—your birthright—because of my petty prejudices, and for all of that..." He glanced around to the Sluagh mother, then knelt down at Skilurus's feet. "...I ask for your forgiveness."

The kid's eyes widened, and he beamed. "Absolutely, Ursus. Absolutely. You have my utmost forgiveness! Thank you!"

"What are you doing, Ursus?" Longinus growled, shoving his spear point into King's back.

King whipped around, batting the spear away, with a sweep of his arms. Longinus recovered quickly, spinning the spear in the air, and leveling the tip once more at him.

"If I'm being forced to do this," King said, his voice unnaturally soft, "then I'm going to take a moment to make right just a few of my wrongs." He turned around to face Rhona. "We've only just met. I can't think of anything I've done personally to you, but I regret the way you and your adoptive people have been treated by the empire I have chosen to fight for all these years. The Romans have not been kind to the peoples of Britannia—especially the Welsh—and for that, I'm truly sorry."

The woman's eyes continued to be as inscrutable as they'd ever been, but with a slight dip of her head, he knew he had her forgiveness.

Longinus hissed. His impatience was wearing thin, but King ignored it, and he stepped over to Polycarp. With an apologetic nod, he smiled down at the rotund clergyman.

"Padre."

"Ursus Rex."

"I think in all my travels and of all my companions, I've been with you the longest."

"Nearly thirty years, I believe." The priest chuckled. "Of course, I was only a youth when I set out to find the *other* centurion that could not be killed. I aimed to test that claim for myself." He paused. "I am truly glad I was wrong about you, Ursus."

"So am I, Padre. But I do owe you many apologies. So many, in fact, I can't name them all. But the chief among them is this...I should have trusted you more. Should have listened to your wisdom, whether I believe in your God or not. There is no question in my mind that you are among the wisest of men I've ever met, and I've too often discounted what you've had to say as superstition and hocus pocus."

"Hocus...pocus?"

"You know what I mean."

"I do. And you are most certainly forgiven." The priest gave King a sly wink. "No matter what happens here today... or who you choose...you are always, most assuredly forgiven."

King gave a slight bow of thanks, then looked directly into the wide, sky-blue eyes of Clarese, hanging on to Polycarp's neck as he continued to hold the girl.

"Enough!" Longinus shouted. "Choose now, or we will do it for you!"

King didn't take his gaze off the girl. "Last one, then I'll make my choice."

"I do not know what you are up to, King," the mother said. *"But whatever it is, it will not work. You are destined to join us. Your essence will change us...make us immortal. And you will most assuredly embrace us this very day."*

King reached out and took Clarese from Polycarp, cradling her on his hip. He brushed strands of her hair from her eyes, and he smiled down at her. "You okay?"

She nodded.

"Do you understand what's happening here right now?"

Another nod. Her eyes were beginning to redden, as a prismatic dome of water formed in the corners. She was obviously fighting back the urge to cry.

"Do you? Forgive me, that is?"

A third nod, followed by a weak smile. She brushed a tear away with her arm. "There is nothing to forgive. You will do what you must. And I will do what I must."

Her words surprised King. "The only thing you have to do is stay in Polycarp's arms. Stay safe. I want you...no, I *need* you to stay safe. You understand me?"

As he waited for the girl to respond, he felt something warm and wet trickling down his neck from where her arms wrapped around him. Curious, he took one of her arms and looked at it. A stream of crimson poured down her arm from a round wound in the center of her wrist. "What the hell?" He wheeled around to face Longinus. "You said none of them would be harmed!"

The Roman shook his head. "We had nothing to do with this."

King looked back at Clarese. Now, beads of blood had blossomed across her brow and were streaming down her cheeks like tears. "Clarese, what's happening?"

He looked over at Polycarp, tears now coming from his weary eyes.

"As she said, Ursus. She must do what she must." The bishop placed a hand on King's shoulder. "Let her go."

King wasn't sure what was happening. His plan wasn't going at all how he'd hoped. Gain everyone in his life's forgiveness of the sins he'd committed toward them. Remove guilt. Overcome the Sluagh's hold on him and do what he did best. But this? He hadn't expected this. The girl was sick. Hemorrhaging from her forehead and wrists—he looked down at her feet, and they were bleeding as well.

A stigmata? Is that what's happening?

But that made no sense. From what he'd heard, stigmatas—physical manifestations of the wounds of Christ—only occurred in the most fanatical of Christian believers. He'd always believed it was nothing more than Catholic superstition; hoaxes perpetuated by believers who wanted to be seen as more spiritual than their peers. But Clarese was no Roman Catholic. The Siluran tribes were pagan. They most certainly weren't Christian.

"Jack Sigler. I need to do this."

King blinked.

Had Clarese just called him by his real name?

"Beyof, please," she said, this time using Rhona's name for him. "Let me down."

He turned to Longinus, whose face seemed just as surprised as his own. Scared even. The massive Sluagh blob in the center of the room seemed to shudder as its bulk swelled, then deflated in rapid, fearful rhythms.

King spun to face Rhona, hoping for her support. But her head dropped, her eyes focusing on the stone floor.

Then, he felt Clarese's hand on his stubbly chin. It was warm. Soft. So very small. He looked at her. The blood continued to pour down her face.

"You are," she said, "now and always, forgiven, Beyof."

There was a pinch at the base of King's neck the moment she spoke the words. For the first time in centuries, he felt whole. At peace with his life. With his path. And though he still missed Sara and Fiona—as well as his brothers and sisters in the Chess Team—he somehow knew they would all be together again.

There was something else, he noticed. The voices. The incessant murmurings of Sluagh voices had stopped. In recent days, since becoming infected, he'd learned to tune them out. But they were always there. Now, their abject silence was deafening.

His plan had worked after all. He'd been set free of his guilt and the parasite attached to his spine was no longer able to combat his heightened immune system. He reached his hand back to a painful itch. Felt something squirm between his fingers. He took hold and pulled, easing it out. Free of the creature, he tossed it on the ground and stepped on its wriggling form.

"You are free," Clarese said. The streams of blood were drying, crusting over the contours of her little face. "Now, let me down. Let me do what I came to do."

He hesitated, but a nod from Polycarp stilled his nerves. He set her down on her feet.

"What is this?" Longinus asked, his eyes wide. "What are you doing?"

Clarese stepped up to the Roman, and smiled up at him. "I told you once already...you are forgiven, as well. He does not hold you responsible. You can let go of your guilt. You can be free, like Beyof."

Longinus shook his head while taking a single step back.

"No. No. No," he muttered. He grasped the spear with both hands and held it in front of him, as if blocking a mighty blow.

"She's right," King said, though he kept his distance. He didn't want to spook the madman while he was so close to the girl. "You can be free. Then, we can end your torment once and for all."

"No." His voice was weak. Almost a question. He glanced over at the Sluagh mother, still pulsing in a rhythmic beat. Its innumerable arms writhed throughout the chamber with each increasing beat. "No."

Then, Clarese closed in on Longinus, spread her arms, and wrapped them around his leg.

"You are forgiven for *this*, as well." Her words were whispered. King and Longinus were the only ones in the chamber who could have heard it. But it had its effect before King could even process what it meant.

"No!" Longinus screamed, shoving the girl away from him, and thrusting the tip of his spear directly into her tiny chest.

26

Clarese crumpled to the floor when Longinus yanked the spear out of her with a snarl. Blood—so much blood—pooled underneath her. It seeped into her hair. Soaked into her sackcloth dress. The stigmata no longer visible amid the gore. King could do nothing but stare at her now lifeless body.

He'd seen his share of death in his time. Seen children of various ages cut down before they'd had a chance to experience life. He was a warrior, after all, and death was part of a warrior's life. But this? It made no sense. He'd seen her still the Sluagh with a single word. Seen her calm Longinus's madness with a simple smile. So what had happened now? Why hadn't it worked?

A wave of nausea swept through him, and he was unable to process the loss. He felt numb. Detached from his own mind. And from the look of it, Longinus was experiencing something similar. The Roman, his eyes nearly as wide as his gaping mouth, stared down at the carnage he'd caused. And he dropped to his knees as he began to shake. He dropped the spear, wrapped his arms around his chest and shivered. Then, he wailed, tears streaming down his face in waves.

"W-what have I done?" he muttered.

But his words were drowned by the sound of a snarling howl. King turned to the noise, to see Skilurus's face contort with rage. He tried to lunge at the Roman, but was held in place by a web of tentacles. Then, the unthinkable happened. As King and the others watched on, Skilurus's nose began to stretch. His teeth lengthened to fierce canines, and bristling hair burst from the skin covering his entire body. He howled again, and King winced when the boy's legs, just at the knees, popped out of place and shifted backward.

"What have I done?" Longinus repeated. "I did it again. How could I have done it again?"

Skilurus continued to change. His back stretched out with the sound of popping bones and sinews, and his chest expanded beyond what should have been anatomically possible for a human being. Growling, he flexed his fingers, and was rewarded with an arsenal of three-inch claws that extended out from his fingertips. A moment later, his wolf-like eyes swiveled across the chamber until they fell on Longinus, and he snarled. Thick streams of saliva cascaded past his jaws and down his fur-covered neck.

Then, the wolf-creature standing on its hind quarters before them raised up its arms, and brought them down over the tentacle bonds. Its nails slashed through the decomposing tissue with a single sweep, releasing all of the captives from the Sluagh's hold. And with another snarl, Skilurus lunged toward the weeping Longinus.

"Skil, no!" King shouted. But the moment Skilurus's feet left the floor, three goblin Sluagh dropped from the ceiling above, and landed on his back. With a canine squeal, the Neuri rolled onto his back, throwing the imp-like creatures off him. He then leapt to his feet, and grabbed the closest goblin by the scruff of the neck, and hurled it headlong into the stone wall.

Ignoring the danger, Polycarp, now free of his bonds, scrambled over to Clarese's side, and checked for signs of life.

"Rhona," King barked. "Watch the door. Make sure no more Sluagh get in."

Though her eyes were red with tears over the loss of her charge, she straightened at his commands. She scooped up King's sword from the ground, and made for the tunnel entrance.

As Skilurus battled with the goblins and the bishop tended the fallen girl, King walked over to Longinus, and stooped to one knee. He wrestled with his hatred of the man. Struggled against the impulse not to snap his neck here and now. But Clarese had made it quite clear. She had seemed to know what would happen. Her last words had been those of forgiveness over what he was about to do.

"You know, our journey here will not end the way you expect." Her words the night before came rushing back to

him. *"You will suffer great loss. A loss that you cannot quite explain that will lead you to be tormented by horrible grief for years to come."*

She knew even then what was going to happen, yet she came anyway.

"Longinus," King said, above the chaotic noise of the werewolf's wrath. "She knew. She knew what you were going to do and she forgave you."

"I killed her." He stared down at his hands, now soiled with her blood. "How many innocents have died because of me?"

King shook his head. "They died *for* you. You're forgiven."

The worms jutting out from the Roman's skin elongated. Boil-like nodules popped up across his face and neck with each breath.

"Longinus, your guilt. Your guilt is feeding them. Strengthening them. Let it go."

The former centurion shot a glare at King. His sclera were now completely red, as capillaries burst from within his eyes. "The only salvation for me, Ursus, is death." He craned his head and found Skilurus, just as he savagely ripped the last goblin Sluagh in two. "Death," Longinus muttered. "Will be a welcome relief."

He then leapt to his feet, turned to face the wolf-beast, and ran headlong toward him.

"Skilurus, don't kill him!" King shouted. But he didn't know if the creature who was once his young protégé could even understand him at this point. In all the years he'd known of the Neuri, he'd never heard of a single one physically transforming like this before. But for the moment, it was the least of his problems. King knew he had to end this. Now.

He rushed over to where the spear had been dropped, and picked it up. Then he lifted the spear and examined the tip. A fresh sample of blood streamed down over the rusted tip, covering the much older crimson stains that tarnished it years before. For a half-second, King simply stared at it. Fresh innocent blood covering more innocent blood from a century before.

But he didn't have any more time to process it. After picking up the spear, a horrible, bone-jarring wail erupted throughout the chamber. Like a warning siren, the noise warbled and screeched at a volume loud enough to make ears bleed.

"Beyof!" Rhona shouted from the doorway. "They are coming!"

Without waiting for a response, the huntress hefted King's sword and dashed from sight into the hallway beyond.

Polycarp, now cradling Clarese in his arms, looked up at King. "Finish this, Ursus. Finish it now!"

With only one clear option left, King lifted the spear and spun to face the huge amorphous creature, the mother of all this chaos. All this death. All this destruction. As he thought about it, he felt consumed with a rage beyond anything he'd experienced before. An anger over every failure he'd had. Every life he'd been unable to save. Every bad decision he'd made.

And then there was Clarese. A little girl he hardly knew. An orphan he'd been reluctant to befriend for fear of losing her like he had so many before. An innocent child overfilled with nothing but compassion and love, and now her life was snuffed out forever as a mere afterthought by this demonic creature.

"No more," he growled before charging the Sluagh mother with the spear held high. But before he could reach her, six sets of serpentine arms shot out from all directions, wrapping around his torso and jerking him from the floor. Two more tentacles constricted around his spear-wielding arm, shaking the weapon loose from his grip. Then, as one, each of the tooth-filled mouths on the tips of each arm clamped onto his flesh. Their fangs dug deep, ripping away at skin, muscle and even bone.

His body spasmed as each of the mouths excreted dozens of tiny larvae, each wriggling their way into the openings and winding their way through his body. This time, however, it was evident that the Sluagh had no intention of using his body as a host. As each of the maggots wormed their way through his system, they tore through him like termites in an old dilapidated house. King felt them chewing away at his organs. Swarming his intestines, his lungs and his heart. Eating him alive, from the inside out. Tweaking his DNA as they moved, undoing the immortal concoction given to him by Alexander centuries ago. They were turning him mortal, and killing him one organ at a time.

Since the destruction of the parasite lodged to his spine, King's immune system had already begun to surge back to its former state, but he wasn't sure whether it would be enough to fend off these new intruders before it was too late. Then, there was the intense agony—like hundreds of microscopic saw blades shaving away at his insides.

He screamed, but only Polycarp seemed to hear him. The old priest noticing King's predicament, laid Clarese's head gently on the ground, scrambled to his feet and ran for the spear, now resting on the floor. But before he could pick it up, another set of tentacles lashed out, and threw the bishop aside, as if he was nothing more than a feather on the wind.

"Padre!" King shouted, trying to turn his head to see if Polycarp had survived. From his vantage point, where the tentacles held him aloft, he couldn't find the bishop anywhere in the chamber. But he could see Skilurus—still in blood-soaked wolf form—and Rhona battling it out with a wave of Sluagh of various shapes and sizes. Longinus, however, was hardly recognizable. He was in a heap in the corner of the chamber. His armor and cloak had been shed, and now he wore mere rags. Blood pooled under his body similar to how it had gathered under Clarese, and King hoped that the crazed centurion had finally found the peace he'd been seeking for nearly a century.

The tentacles tightened around King's waist, wrenching his attention back to the moment. The pain built to near unbearable levels. Worse, it was moving. Slowly drifting to the center of King's mass. The Sluagh larvae were wandering toward his heart.

And he had no doubt, if they succeeded in consuming every morsel of his body, this time, he would die for good.

27

Polycarp's ears rang as he struggled to push himself off the ground. The blob-like demon that now had Ursus in its web of arms had hit him harder than he'd anticipated. Had nearly taken his head off with the blow. But the Lord had seen fit to spare him yet again, though why, he couldn't say. He could hardly do anything to rectify the situation in which they found themselves.

Uncertain of what to do, he turned to Skilurus, still fighting the horde of Sluagh that had bottlenecked the chamber's entrance. Skilurus. The bishop couldn't understand it. He'd known the boy carried a secret, but he never imagined this. It wasn't just the thick fur that now covered his wide, hunched back or the elongated snout with ferocious fangs glistening with the blood of his enemies. It wasn't the physical transformation that vexed the bishop as much as the change to his demeanor. Skilurus was such a good boy. Kind hearted. Compassionate.

And now?

He watched as the wolf-creature lashed one of the short, squat Sluagh with his unnaturally long claws, slicing it almost in half.

Is he still Skilurus in there? Can he be reasoned with?

The fact that Rhona had no qualms fighting the monsters beside the beast made him think it was possible. After all, he wasn't trying to eviscerate her as he was their attackers.

Polycarp looked back over at Ursus, still struggling against his demonic bonds with all his might. His screams were deafening. The bishop shuddered at the sight of the worm-like mouths digging deeper into the warrior's flesh. The maggot creatures that had warped Longinus's body, were now starting to do the same to Ursus. Their gray-white heads splitting open the skin of his arms, neck and face... writhing with the same rhythm as the monstrous tentacled creature at the room's core. Blood cascaded from the sores opening all over Ursus's body.

The man, the centurion he'd come to respect and care for like his very own son, was going to die. Where countless swords, arrows and nooses had failed to end the strange man's life, these demon worms were sure to succeed.

Surely, this is not how it is supposed to end, Lord, he prayed. *The girl. Your Christophany's sacrifice was supposed to end this once and for all, was she not?*

He thought back to the conversation he'd had with Rhona three nights before, outside the walls of Isca Silurum. The huntress had told him an unimaginable tale about the girl. No. 'Girl' wasn't quite right, was it? She was, after all, nearly seventy-five years old. And despite what Clarese had believed, no one knew who her parents were. She'd simply wandered into Celwyn one day, seventy-five years before. She had a wisdom unmatched by anyone within leagues of the village...wisdom that made her the greatest healer anyone had ever seen.

She had also never aged. Physically, and in many ways, mentally. She had knowledge that surpassed even the greatest thinkers of Rome and Greece, but she couldn't remember anything about her own life beyond a few short years. Rhona had been charged with caring for her and was forced to pledge to keep the girl's secret from her, lest the news be too great a shock for her.

Polycarp, in his hubris, believed he'd cracked the mystery. The girl had appeared at roughly the same time that Longinus's spear—blood of the Risen Christ still staining its tip—was buried within this stone megalith. He'd seen how the Sluagh had responded to her. Watched as they quivered under the aura of her innocence. And so, he'd speculated that Clarese was none other than a Christophany. A manifestation of Christ outside of the context of his own timeline. It was common enough during the Old Covenant period. Surely, it was still possible...

He glanced down at Clarese's lifeless body and frowned. She'd died. A pointless death. Her sacrifice had accomplished nothing at all. They would all soon be following her, and there wasn't a blessed thing that could be done.

A groan to the bishop's left caught his attention. He turned to investigate just in time, to see a blood-covered mess streak past him, howling with a fury that nearly dropped him to his knees, as it rushed toward the mother beast.

28

King's vision was darkening. They had reached his heart and were already gnawing away at it. His chest spasmed as he tried to take a breath, but he was prevented from doing so by a rush of blood exploding like a geyser from his mouth when he exhaled. The mercy of it all was that the larvae had apparently eaten away at the majority of his nerve endings. The pain had receded to something akin to tolerable, making it easier for him to struggle against the tentacles holding him in place.

I won't give up. He wasn't sure the mother could hear his thoughts anymore, now that their connection had been severed, but he wanted her to understand it anyway. *I'll never give up. I've been dead before. I have no fear of it now. So just know, you will die by my hand before this is all over.*

If the Sluagh mother heard him, she offered no indication. Instead, she continued to pulse and throb with her incessant rhythmic beat, as her children glutted themselves on her enemy's insides.

King craned his head. Skilurus and Rhona were holding their own. The wave of Sluagh creatures appeared to be thinning, but his companions were far too consumed with the battle to lend him a hand. He caught a glimpse of Polycarp in his peripheral vision. The old priest was pushing himself up from the ground, wiping a smear of blood from his brow. He seemed dazed, but otherwise uninjured.

He's the best of all of us. Hopefully, he'll survive, even if the rest of us don't.

He watched the priest for a moment longer. Then, an intense surge of searing pain shot down his arms and legs. Another streaked up his neck, radiating toward his jaw. His eyes dimmed further. The world grew hazy around him. What little he could see of it, spun wildly about, filling him with nausea.

He was having a heart attack. Or rather, his heart was nearly consumed by the maggots feasting within him.

Unable to contain his agony, King screamed. He screamed louder than he could remember ever screaming before. The pain was excruciating. But more than that, he screamed because he had failed. He had been unable to destroy the abomination in front of him, and now the Sluagh would go out into the world unchecked. Unhindered. Untold thousands of people would die.

And just as his vision was dimming to complete blackness, a crimson blur—distorted and grotesque—slammed its body into the Sluagh mother with all its might.

Skilurus?

Before he could figure out who the new attacker was, he dropped to the ground, now released from his tentacle bonds, and died.

"Mother!"

King heard the scream before he was aware of anything else.

"You did this to me!"

The voice sounded strange. Unearthly. Like a thousand voices yelling in unison. A deep-throated roar of a voice.

"You will pay for what you have done!"

King blinked. His breathing was stable again. He was no longer coughing up blood. And if he concentrated enough, he could feel the slightest trace of a pulse beating in his own forehead.

There was a crashing sound just ahead of him. Then another scream.

He tried to look up, but the moment King lifted his head, he exploded in a round of hacking coughs. Bits of maggots spewed from his lips, falling lifeless to the floor. His throat burned as the desiccated larvae made their way up his larynx to be expelled by his coughing fit. He reached out his hands, trying to stabilize himself amid the spinning world he now found himself in, and he touched something cold and solid.

The spear.

Just within reach. If only he had strength enough to grab it.

"You should never have made me kill her, Mother!" The voice continued. "She did not deserve to die! She was the only person who never seemed to judge me."

More crashing. More growls. More screams. King couldn't place where any of these noises were coming from within the chamber. He was aware that Skilurus and Rhona were still battling it out with the never-ending army of Sluagh somewhere. He could hear the soft murmurings of Polycarp in prayer. And then, there was the mournful voice crying out to his mother.

Longinus? No, can't be.

Last he looked, Skilurus had torn the Roman apart.

King found just enough strength to lift his head. The sight nearly sent him in another fit of convulsions. The two-legged creature pounding huge fists into the Sluagh mother was no longer a man—at least, not in the technical sense of the word. It no longer wore any skin. Its body was now little more than a mass of exposed muscle tissue wrapped around cartilage and bone. The bones themselves were broken in several places; their sharpened points jutting out of arms, legs and even the back. It was larger than any human King had ever seen, but not quite as big as the watchers who kept guard outside. The worms and elongated tentacles were still there, though they were now more plentiful than ever before.

In a gut-wrenching revelation, King knew with certainty that he was looking at Longinus's final Sluagh form.

'And then, after you think you have defeated them, you will still have to face the Grundling.' Clarese's words came to him yet again. Longinus had indeed been killed by Skilurus. And the Grundling, a creature born out of the earth—or under it—had arisen to take his place. This was the creature that Clarese had warned King about. The monster that he would eventually have to face.

If we can make it out of here alive.

King grunted and pushed himself up from the ground, grabbing the spear as he rose. His shoulders sagged. His legs wobbled. Though he was living again, he had not quite fully revived. But his eyes were now clear, and his grip was strong enough to raise the weapon that would one day become known as the Spear of Destiny.

He watched as Longinus tore at the mother with his bare hands. His nails digging deep into her decomposing flesh, pulling it apart piece by piece. Her tentacles lashed out at the skinless man, embedding their teeth into him with the vicious ferocity of piranhas. And yet, he continued to ravage her, ignoring some of the tentacle attacks, and countering some with the tendrils now jutting from his back, shoulders and chest.

King took a breath. Hefted the spear above his shoulder, then hurled it straight at the Mother Sluagh's center mass. His aim was true, and the spear's tip plunged deep inside the enormous creature.

Then, everything stopped.

Longinus looked down at the weapon, then turned and glared at King. The other Sluagh ceased their fighting, and turned toward their mother in reverent silence. Even Skilurus—already transforming back to his youthful countenance—and Rhona spun around to see what had just transpired. Only Polycarp's mumbling prayers could be heard within the chamber.

Seconds ticked by.

One. Two. Three.

Then, the giant tentacled beast began to shudder and squeal. Its arms flailed, rending themselves away from the walls and ceiling. They lashed about, forcing the humans to stoop to avoid being struck. The other Sluagh, however, didn't notice. Their eyes had grown blank. Their stolen muscles and corrupted flesh went slack, and in unison, they fell to the floor. Then, the Mother began to hiss. Her remaining flesh began to boil and pop. Geysers of black blood oozed from the wounds created by Longinus's vengeful attack. She warbled and wretched, her rhythmic pulse now erratic and ill-defined.

Was it the blood that killed it? King wondered. *Or simply a mortal blow?* In either case, his DNA had not bolstered the Sluagh as they had hoped it would. Though they could manipulate the human form and give it a semblance of life for a time, they were far from human themselves. Perhaps his DNA simply wasn't compatible?

Longinus's lidless eyes gazed down at her for a moment, then he looked over at King. "We are now even," he said with his thunderstorm voice. "You and yours should leave now. These tunnels will soon crumble."

King stared back at him. "What will happen to you?" His question was a loaded one. He was really asking if King needed to be concerned about what Longinus would do now, and he knew the Roman understood.

"I will do what I have always done. I will run. Run to a secluded place. A place far from any people, and live out my days."

King nodded.

"Know this, Ursus. What happened here today does not make us allies. It does not make us friends. You killed my mother."

"But..."

Longinus Grundling held up a hand. "I am a Son of Cain. A killer of family. You took away my birthright in that act. It was my right alone to end her existence. You took that from me." He let out a low growl. "I let you live today. The next time I see you, I will not hesitate to finish what my mother started."

King pondered that a few moments, then nodded his understanding. He stepped forward and pulled the spear from the lifeless husk of the Sluagh without concern Longinus would protest. With a last look back, King stalked out of the chamber following his friends, who were carrying the body of Clarese.

EPILOGUE

Heorot Hall, Denmark
A.D. 542

The creature stalked through the shadows, making its way over the snow swept hills of the kingdom of Hrothgar, vexed beyond measure. It had come to this place, centuries before, to get away from the world. Get away from humans. Now, the puny king of the Danes, in all his hubris, had done the unthinkable. He'd built that infernal mead hall, Heorot. A den of debauchery for the king's warriors. The sound of their merriment was a constant insult to the creature.

The creature grew to loathe these people. Hated their revelry. Despised their very happiness. So, in recent months, it had taken to nighttime raids. On those evenings where the festivities were the most raucous, the creature would sweep into the Hall and decimate all who still remained...until finally, at long last, King Hrothgar had boarded up the doors to Heorot once and for all. There'd been peace in the land for weeks. Months, perhaps. The creature found itself happy once more, and had given up its raids—choosing instead, to resume its life in the caverns eight miles north of the Hall.

Then, tonight, its blessed peace had once again been interrupted by the sound of raucous merry making. Echoes of laughter had rolled their way over the hills to its home. The jarring twang of the lyre danced over the waters and into its cave. And the acrid stench of ale and mead burned at its nostrils like acid. The creature could take it no longer. It had no idea what had prompted the idiot king to reopen the doors to that damned Hall, but he would ensure they never opened again. Not after this night. Tonight, it would destroy every last person under Hrothgar's reign.

And so, the creature stole through the village in the dead of night, until it came to the doors of Heorot.

Unexpectedly, there was a man standing in front, cloaked in fur with a hood covering his head. The man held a sword. A familiar sword, though the creature couldn't quite place where it had seen the blade before.

"I hear you're called Grendel now," the man said.

Strange. The man didn't seem to be afraid of the creature at all.

"And what might they call thee?" Grendel's thunderous voice boomed. Its fingers flexed, curling into two sledge-hammer-sized fists.

The man stepped forward, tossed his sword tip into the deep snow and pulled back his cloak.

The creature snarled. "Uuurrssuusss."

He smiled at Grendel, but shook his head. "Not any-more," he said. "I go by something else now. You can call me Beowulf."

The monster who had once been Longinus snarled and then opened its hands wide. "Have you asked yourself what happened to all the dead? The abandoned bodies did not go to the pier, they came to me. And I preserved them with the gift you gave us—longevity." The monster grinned, worms dripping from its mouth. A hulking form stepped out of the darkness, gripping a battle axe. It was followed by another. And another. Warriors all, consumed by the Sluagh. "We have taken a new name as well."

"Speak it," Beowulf said. "Before I cut you down."

"We are Draugr."

KING TIMELINE

"He fought in wars. Led armies. Staged coups. Defeated evil. He'd lived lives as vagrant nobodies, as revered heroes and demigods, as quiet farmers and famous warriors, in every part of the world."

2006 Events of *Prime*

2009 Events of *Pulse*

2010 Events of *Instinct*

2011 Events of *Threshold*

2011 Events of *Callsign: King*

2011 Events of *Callsign King 2: Underworld*

2011 Events of *Callsign: Deep Blue* (epilogue)

2011 Events of *Callsign King 3: Blackout*

2012 Events of *Ragnarok*

2013 Events of *Omega*—King was sent back in time

799 BC King and Alexander returned to the past in Ancient Carthage

799 BC King's first death & resurrection

795 BC King and Alexander fought Samnites in Campania

780 BC Etruria, Alexander returned to his dimension; King was recognized as Perseus

776 BC King was at First Olympic Games in Olympia

776 BC King lived in rural Greece for ten years

766 BC King lived in Athens for 97 years

669 BC King overthrew a despot outside Athens, and took the name Achelous

612 BC King fought animal-human hybrids

595 BC King fought the Minotaur in Crete

577 BC King was a Pirate and owed King Jian of the Zhou Dynasty money

576 BC King was in Persia for events of *Guardian*

100 BC King was eaten repeatedly by werewolves in the Carpathian Mountains

AD 73 King met Polycarp, Bishop of Smyrna

AD 102 Events of *Centurion*

AD 542 King was in Denmark and slew Grendel, using the name Beowulf

AD 577 King was in suspended animation for thirty years

AD 613 King lived on a vineyard in Italy

AD 647 King lived as a fisherman in Macedonia

AD 1242 King was digested by a large predator, location unknown

AD 1453 King served at the Fall of Constantinople as a Roman Legionnaire

AD 1493 King traveled with Ponce De Leon for twenty years

AD 1588 King was at the destruction of the Roanoke settlement

AD 1627 King searched for the Fountain of Youth; unknown whether he found it

AD 1663 King's pirate crew took a slave ship at Charles Town and freed the slaves

AD 1674 King's *Presley's Hound* crew of the Forgotten battled giant creatures

AD 1675 King sealed himself in a coffin on Kavo Zile island to wait out time

AD 1775 Events of *Patriot*

AD 1776 King fought in the American Revolutionary War as a Minuteman

AD 1939 King was in the Himalayas

AD 1970 Buzz Aldrin gives King the wristwatch he wore on the moon

AD 2012 King infiltrated Endgame HQ, stole plans for technology in *Ragnarok*

AD 2013 Events of *Omega*—Ancient King rejoined Chess Team

AD 2014 Events of *Savage*

AD 2015 Events of *Cannibal*

AD 2015 Events of *Endgame*

AD 2015 Events of "Show of Force"

AD 2016 Events of *Empire*

ABOUT THE AUTHOR

Jeremy Robinson is the international bestselling author of over fifty novels and novellas including *MirrorWorld*, *XOM-B*, *Island 731*, *SecondWorld*, the Jack Sigler thriller series, and *Project Nemesis*, the highest selling, original (non-licensed) kaiju novel of all time. He's known for mixing elements of science, history and mythology, which has earned him the #1 spot in Science Fiction and Action-Adventure, and secured him as the top creature feature author.

Robinson is also known as the bestselling horror writer, Jeremy Bishop, author of *The Sentinel* and the controversial novel, *Torment*. In 2015, he launched yet another pseudonym, Jeremiah Knight, for two post-apocalyptic Science Fiction series of novels. Robinson's works have been translated into thirteen languages.

His series of Jack Sigler / Chess Team thrillers, starting with *Pulse*, is in development as a film series, helmed by Jabbar Raisani, who earned an Emmy Award for his design work on HBO's *Game of Thrones*. Robinson's original kaiju character, Nemesis, was also adapted into a comic book through publisher American Gothic Press in association with *Famous Monsters of Filmland*, with artwork and covers by renowned Godzilla artists Matt Frank and Bob Eggleton.

Born in Beverly, MA, Robinson now lives in New Hampshire with his wife and three children.

Visit Jeremy online at www.bewareofmonsters.com.

ABOUT THE AUTHOR

J. Kent Holloway is the international bestselling author of six paranormal thrillers, including his highly acclaimed Ezekiel Crane series, as well as his forensic thriller, *Clean Exit*. He's also written his first installment of the Baron Tombstone adventures in the shared pirate world series, Tattered Sails.

Kent has more than twenty years of experience working as a forensic death investigator within two different medical examiner offices in the state of Florida. He's also worked as a private investigator, a high school teacher of criminal justice, and a newspaper reporter covering the crime beat. When he's not writing, designing book covers, or investigating deaths, he spends much of his spare time investigating ghosts and cryptids throughout northeast Florida.

Find Kent at his website: www.kenthollowayonline.com.

Made in the USA
San Bernardino, CA
15 January 2018